The
Outlandish
Adventures
of Liberty Aimes

The Outlandish Adventures
of Liberty Aimes

kelly easton

illustrated by greg swearingen

A Yearling Book

Text copyright © 2009 by Kelly Easton
Illustrations copyright © 2009 by Greg Swearingen

All rights reserved. Published in the United States by Yearling, an imprint of Random House Children's Books, a division of Random House, Inc., New York. Originally published in hardcover in the United States by Wendy Lamb Books, an imprint of Random House Children's Books, a division of Random House, Inc., New York, in 2009.

Yearling and the jumping horse design are registered trademarks of Random House, Inc.

Visit us on the Web! www.randomhouse.com/kids

Educators and librarians, for a variety of teaching tools, visit us at www.randomhouse.com/teachers

Library of Congress Cataloging-in-Publication Data
Easton, Kelly.
The outlandish adventures of Liberty Aimes / Kelly Easton.
p. cm.
Summary: Ten-year-old Libby Aimes escapes her prison-like home by using a strange concoction of her father's, then tries to make her way to the boarding school of her dreams, aided by various people and animals.
ISBN 978-0-375-83771-5 (hardcover) — ISBN 978-0-375-93771-2 (Gibraltar lib. bdg.) — ISBN 978-0-375-83772-2 (pbk.) — ISBN 978-0-375-89256-1 (ebook) [1. Runaways—Fiction. 2. Human-animal communication—Fiction. 3. Family problems—Fiction. 4. Inventors—Fiction. 5. Adventure and adventurers—Fiction.] I. Title.
PZ7.E13155Out 2009
[Fic]—dc22
2008022119

Printed in the United States of America

10 9 8 7 6 5 4 3 2 1

First Yearling Edition 2011

Random House Children's Books supports the First Amendment and celebrates the right to read.

For Randall Easton Wickham, and for Isaac, and
for my family

Libby Aimes

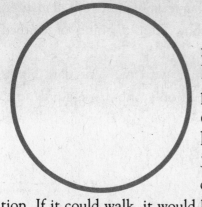nce upon a time like now, and in a place like here, there existed a crooked house. The house at 33 Gooch Street was decrepit beyond description. If it could walk, it would limp. If it could talk, it would stutter. If it could smile, it would have rotting teeth. You get the picture.

The back of the house was surrounded by high concrete walls and choked by vines. The front yard had only a picnic bench split in two by lightning, and a row of thorny bushes that never produced a rose.

Insects had fled 33 Gooch, leaving behind their nests' empty catacombs, their webs' dusty strands. Only the mosquitoes came each evening, undiscerning bloodsuckers that they are.

People also avoided the house. The postman delivered the mail at a trot. Trick-or-treaters crossed the street, dashing to number 34, the bright yellow house where the man handed out gummy worms.

That man was the only person who knew that inside 33 Gooch lived a family. He knew because he watched the house with great curiosity.

The family was a couple and their only daughter, Liberty, nicknamed Libby, after a brand of canned vegetables.

Libby Aimes was small, with two long dark braids and pale skin. She owned only one dress, a gray one, with big pockets to hold her cooking utensils and cleaning supplies.

Although she was ten, she was not in any grade, like you might be. Her parents had never allowed her to go to school. They told the school officials that she would be "homeschooled." Usually, that's a fine thing. For Libby, though, it meant that she was locked up all day, waiting on her parents hand and foot, dodging their insults like a beleaguered catcher.

Some people have names that suit them exactly. Like Lilac, for someone who smells nice. Or Jock, for a boy who's good at sports. Libby's real name, Liberty, was kind of a joke. She was a prisoner in her own house. It was good that her parents always called her by her nickname. She had never heard her real name pass their lips.

Libby's mother, Sal, had grown up at 33 Gooch, but she never talked about that. What she talked about was how, because of Libby, she was now fat, married to a dud, and stuck in her life.

Libby never understood the connection between herself and her mother's extreme tubbiness. Her mother was fat, Libby knew, because she ate nonstop. Each day Sal consumed thirty-two pieces of fried French toast, seven pounds of fried clams, sixteen fried hot dogs, two fried chickens, twenty fried hamburgers, six platters of French fries, three platters of fried noodles, a pie (not fried), six ice cream sundaes, and a variety of other foods. Libby cooked these meals, so she knew the numbers.

The only thing she didn't cook for her mother was the buttergoo pudding Sal consumed three times a day. Libby's father, Mal, cooked it. Mal told Libby that if she dared to taste a drop, he would "teach her a lesson." It was something he often said, although Libby had yet to figure out what the lesson was.

As unpleasant as Sal was, Liberty's father was worse. Mal (which means "evil" in French) was thin as a thread, and so tall that he whacked his head walking through doorways. The constant stooping made him look crooked. Unlike Sal, Mal barely ate a morsel; he said that eating was a sign of bad character.

Mal was the only one who ever left the house. During the day, he sold insurance. "People are terrified of disasters," he said. "I remind them about landslides, tornadoes, hurricanes, earthquakes, tsunamis, fires, termite infestations, carpenter bees, bedbugs, bad guys, and wild goats on rampages. Then I sell them insurance."

Mal was crooked inside as well as outside. If a disaster really did befall one of his customers, Mal had tricks to avoid paying the claims. Libby had heard him numerous times, shouting into the phone he kept in his pocket. "Read the fine print!"

The fine print was writing at the bottom of contracts, so small you could only see it with a magnifying glass. It said that the insurance company was not responsible for any disasters that occurred between the days of Sunday and Saturday.

This made the policy worthless. Oh, Mal was happy when he got to tell some homeless or injured person, "Read the fine print."

Have you ever had a ripe apple fresh from the tree? It is delicious: crunchy and sweet. But once in a while, you bite into an apple that is mushy and vile. Parents are much the same as apples. Most of them are perfectly lovely, but occasionally you find one that is rotten. Mal was such a bad apple. He also smelled rotten, since he bathed only during months that had a Z in them. Baths cost too much, he said, but Libby figured he just liked being filthy and gross to match his personality.

In addition to making Libby do all the cooking and cleaning, Mal made her pry up the bricks on the back patio and then lay them again, even in the winter, to teach her a lesson. She had to wax his shoes, cut his toenails, groom his mustache, and brush his teeth; his breath smelled like a warthog's (at least, that was what she imagined).

"Do you know why you do what I say?" Mal asked Libby ten or twenty times a day.

She was too frightened to answer, but he always answered for her.

"Because I'm a friggin' genius, and you are a zero."

Some people, when told they're a zero, take it to heart and feel like a nothing. But Libby was too smart for that. She knew that a zero was a fine, round thing. *Put a zero on any number*, she thought, *and it becomes more valuable.*

Sal also called Mal "the genius." She'd say, "The genius is stinking up the bathroom again." Or, "The genius thinks we can pay the mortgage with ideas." For no matter how many people "the genius" cheated, Libby's family was always dead broke.

The reason Mal called *himself* a friggin' genius was that he invented things; at least, he tried to. Every night, after he came home from work, he went into his basement laboratory to invent.

Libby had been informed that if she ever went down there, she would be poisoned by gases and punished by torture. The house would crumble to the ground, burying her underneath it. Worse, she would be taught a lesson. "Curiosity killed the cat," Mal told her. "It can do the same to you."

Luckily for Libby, she didn't believe him. If she had, there would be no book. You would be holding empty pages in your hands.

She didn't believe him because he had never said anything truthful or done anything trustworthy. Also, they had never had a cat. How could curiosity have killed it?

Like any child, Libby *was* curious. She was curious about the names of the trees and the movement of the stars. She was curious about life outside.

She was *very* curious about what Mal had in the basement. Many times, she had looked for an extra key to that door, but she had never found it. The only one that seemed to exist was on a key chain looped on Mal's belt. Even when he slept, he wore his clothes (which he rarely changed), the belt firmly attached.

Libby knew from hearing her father talk to Sal that he built contraptions and concocted potions: to grow hair, to peel paint, to alter the weather, to channel lightning, to erase wrinkles.

Each invention, he was convinced, would make him rich. "Know why I want to be rich?" he asked Libby. "So I can put you in boarding school and be rid of you."

However, none of his inventions worked; at least, he said they didn't. They always needed to be "perfected." That never seemed to happen.

Libby wished Mal would get rich. More than anything, she wanted to go to boarding school. Hidden under her mattress she had a collection of school brochures that had come in the mail. Her favorite was for the Sullivan School. That brochure had photos of children riding horses, ice-skating, swimming, and studying on a green lawn. It showed teachers with kind faces and a library with books from ceiling to floor.

One day, Libby promised herself, she would escape, and live up to her *real* name: Liberty.

Jack Sprat

Aside from curiosity, Libby had *hope*. Hope is, of course, the belief that if you are patient and trusting, terrible times will pass and the future will be bright. I am quite old, so I know that hope works, especially when combined with effort.

Although Libby didn't go to school, she had managed to educate herself. From laying the patio bricks, she had learned to count, multiply, divide, and do geometry.

From copying words from food packages onto a shopping list for Mal, she had a clue about reading and writing. She also had a dim memory of Sal teaching her the alphabet and the sound each letter made.

There were no books allowed in the house, or so Libby was told. Even Sal thought Libby should be allowed a book or two, but Mal would say, "I don't want a kid who's smarter than me."

When Libby was six, though, she had made a great discovery.

Like most people who are lazy, Sal watched TV. Her favorite show was *Queen for Once*. It was about women who went on diets and then got to buy new clothes, wear a little crown, and take a cruise. Each episode, a different woman received this makeover, after which she talked about how her life had changed, and cried.

Libby loved it when Sal watched *Queen for Once*, because she could do as she liked for an hour.

One cold, dark winter day, while Sal watched TV, Libby tried the basement door, hoping that Mal had, for once, forgotten to lock it. He never did.

Next, she tiptoed upstairs and snuck into her parents' room. Their window had the best view of the street. Occasionally, she'd see kids walking by. Or she'd look at the yard across the street, at number 34, with its varied trees, flowers, and bushes.

That day, Libby pulled the curtains from the dirty window. But the snow was so heavy that no one was out. The street was as dull as her life. As she tiptoed out of the room, she tripped on the shaggy old rug and fell.

Libby lay there a moment, stunned. Then she noticed something. Just under the bed was a break in the wood floor. She peeled back the rest of the rug. A wide square was cut in the floor, with hinges on one side. What if it led to the basement? She yanked on the door. It opened with a creak. Dust flew into her face. It was just a storage area, a pit in the floor. It didn't lead anywhere. But when the dust cleared, Libby saw that it was filled with books.

Some of the books were quite thick, with so many words they were like ants running across the page. Some were thin. She picked up a bright green one. The cover showed an old lady with glasses riding a giant bird.

"Mot . . . her." Libby tried to sound out the first word. The second word was easier. "Goose." The white bird!

The first page of the goose book had an illustration of a skinny man like Mal and a fat woman like Sal. Slowly, Libby sounded out the words: *Jack Sprat could eat no fat. His wife could eat no lean.*

Someone, somewhere, shared her experience!

She opened another book. This one was about a silly-looking cat wearing a tall hat. She examined the bigger books, which had fewer pictures and more words.

Her mother had grown up in this house. These must have been *her* books. And all of them, it seemed, were for children!

There was a
crooked man

For the four years following her discovery, Libby read whenever she could. She hid books in the bathroom, in the heating vent, under her bed, and in the kitchen behind the canned goods, stealing time from her chores to read.

But one fine spring day, two terrible things happened. The first was that she finished reading the last book. It was *Alice's Adventures in Wonderland*, and it was her favorite.

The second terrible thing was that she overheard a conversation.

It was early morning. As Libby made her way downstairs to fix breakfast, she heard her parents arguing; she stopped on the stairs and listened.

"Nighttime plumbing," Mal was saying. "While people sleep, I'll clean out their pipes. Libby will help me."

"But what will she *do*?"

"She's got skinny arms. She'll stick her hands in the toilets and pull things out. Or if it's a bad case, I'll lower her into the sewer."

"At night?" Sal asked.

"I've got the insurance business during the day. It'll have to be at night."

"But when will she sleep?"

"We'll let her have a couple of hours during the day. It'll teach her a lesson."

"It's against the law," Sal argued. "Ten-year-olds can't work."

"Where she's going to work, no one will see her. I've got it all figured out."

"I don't know," Sal said. "I thought somehow that when I had a child, she would have a *childhood*."

"What use is a childhood? Did anyone ever make money from having a childhood?" Mal's voice got low. "Do you know why she'll do what I say?"

"Because you're a friggin' genius?" said Sal.

"That's right."

"I don't like it."

"Since when do you make decisions around here?"

Libby tiptoed into the kitchen to start Sal's breakfast. Which would be worse? Sticking her hands into toilets or having to be with Mal?

She sighed and pinned her hair on top of her head. Once, her long braids had fallen into the pot of hot oil and it took weeks to remove the smell of fried clams from her hair.

Libby dragged the French toast from the freezer and opened the package. From the enormous pocket of her dress, she pulled tongs to pick up the frozen pieces and drop them into the hot oil. Sal liked her food fried.

"Don't forget to eat your pudding." Mal slammed the door as he left for work.

"Libby!" Sal shouted. "I want clams for breakfast. I'm tired of French toast."

"But I've . . ." Libby didn't finish the sentence. Sal wouldn't care that she was already making French toast. "Okay."

As Libby pulled the pieces of toast from the oil with her tongs, she tried to shut Mal's idea out of her mind. Instead, she thought about *Alice*. What would it be like to fall down a hole and chase a white rabbit? Or go through a mirror into another world and play croquet with a deck of cards?

She thought about all of the wonderful things she'd read: the gingerbread house in the woods, the beanstalk in the sky, the curious monkey, the Munchkins and Emerald City, the talking lion, the dragons, and the magic carpet.

None of those things would happen to her. Her life had always struck her as mean, but now she knew it was even worse: It was boring.

Libby plunged the clams into the pot. Tears dripped down her face, sizzling as they hit the oil.

Nothing ever happened. She had read the last book. There were no more. She could read them again, but there wouldn't be the surprise, the delight of finding out what happened next.

She dumped the clams onto a platter, tasting a couple. That was how she ate, taking a bit while she was cooking.

"Libby!" Sal shrieked. "I'm starving, you slowpoke."

"Coming!"

The plumbing predicament popped into her mind again. She had to find a way out of Mal's terrible plan.

But how?

Worm Man

Libby set Sal's clams on her TV tray. If only they could open the curtains. It was spring outside, but it felt like winter in their house. Always winter, dark and cold.

"Where's my maple syrup?" Sal demanded. "Did you forget I like maple syrup on my clams?"

"Here, Mother. It's right here."

"This better be *real* maple syrup. Mal is working on an invention to make maple syrup right in his laboratory. He thinks it will save money. That's all the loser cares about."

"I was thinking. . . ." Libby sat on the footstool in front of her mother.

"Thinking is a bad idea, if you ask me."

"Wouldn't it be nice to go out?"

"Why would we do that?"

"Well . . ." Libby thought of the garden across the street, but only food would appeal to her mother. "I noticed a plum tree across the street, and some of the fruit has dropped to the ground. We could collect it and I could make a pudding for you."

"Across the street?"

"At number thirty-four. There's a lovely garden, with fruit trees and grapevines and flowers."

"Were you looking outside? You know Mal doesn't allow that." Sal crunched a clam.

"The kitchen curtains are so thin, I couldn't help it."

"Worm Man lives there."

"Worm Man?"

"He studies worms. He's a scientist. Even as a child, he collected worms. I called him Worm Boy then."

"You know him?" As long as Libby could remember, they'd never had company or been to anyone's house.

"I grew up with him." Sal's eyes got watery. "We . . . played together. Did you know that if you cut a worm in two, both sides keep wriggling?"

"I can't believe you know him."

"Stop being a nincompoop and make me a marsh-mallow sundae. These clams taste like fried worms."

Sometimes, when people are horrible to you, you get used to it, and it seems normal. That was what had happened to Libby. Her mom calling her a nincompoop made little impression on her.

She went back to the kitchen. *Worm Man*, she thought. Her mother knew him! What if they could visit?

"What took you so long?" Sal dug her spoon into the huge sundae. "You get lazier every second. This sundae is terrible! Nothing tastes like it's supposed to today." Sal shoved another spoonful into her mouth.

Have you ever heard of a boiling point? It's when a liquid turns from a calm, smooth surface into an angry, bubbling volcano.

After ten years, Libby was at hers. "Don't you want to *do* something, Mother?"

"Like what?"

Go to a park, or a museum, or a library? But she knew Sal didn't want to do any of those things. "Like be one of those ladies on *Queen for Once* who get to buy new clothes and go on a cruise?"

"Too busy." Sal motioned to the sundae.

"Wouldn't you like a *change?*"

Sal pointed her spoon at Libby like a dagger. "You not satisfied with your lot? The good life we give you not enough?"

A pool of tears rose inside of Libby. What was she thinking, trying to talk to her mother?

"Besides," Sal said with a sniff, "I applied to *Queen for Once* two hundred seventeen times. No one even wrote back."

"It could still happen." The pool spilled from Libby's eyes. Usually, she saved her tears for her pillow at night. She'd never cried in front of her parents.

Sal's eyes bugged out. "Wh-what's the matter? I mean . . . y-you can have a sundae if you want. Make a big one. That's okay with me."

Libby was amazed. Sal had never offered her anything before. The idea of making a sundae and eating with her mother quieted her tears. "I'll be right back," Libby said, but she didn't get a chance to go anywhere.

The front door burst open and in stumbled Mal, smelling about seventeen times worse than usual.

Opportunity knocking

"Help!" he cried, and fell on the floor, pounding his fists like a spoiled child.

Sal clamped her hand over her nose. "What happened? Did you fall into a trash heap? Did you step in cow manure? Did someone puke on you on the subway? Did the town dump move into our living room?"

"I was sprayed by a skunk, you moron!" Mal shouted. "And I have to be at work in half an hour."

Although the smell was foul, Libby couldn't help but giggle at the sight of her father, fuming and in need of fumigation, in the living room.

"Why were you bothering a skunk?" Sal asked.

"I wasn't bothering it; I was making a deal with it."

Making a deal with a skunk? Libby thought.

"Do something," Mal shouted. "I can't stand the smell and I have three appointments. Do something or I'll rub it off on you!"

"Libby!" Sal yelled. "Find some canned tomato juice and pour it in a bath for your father."

"I. Don't. Bathe!" Mal said.

"Well, you'll have to. No one will buy insurance from

you smelling like that. And I'm certainly not having anything rubbed on *me*."

Libby ran into the kitchen to look for canned tomato juice. All she could find were two jars of spaghetti sauce. She rushed the jars to the bathroom, ran a bath, and poured the sauce into the tub, along with all of the shampoo she could find.

She smelled rather than heard her father. "Get out," he said. Libby backed all the way out of the bedroom. Mal slammed the door.

There is a scientific theory called chaos theory, which says that small events can create big changes, like a butterfly flapping its wings in Brazil can cause a tornado in Texas.

There is also an old saying that opportunity doesn't knock twice, which is not true. Opportunity knocks many times, just never in the same way.

Libby had overheard that she might have to stick her hands in toilets and be lowered into sewers. She had finished the last book. Her mother had offered her ice cream, which made her feel odd, like she'd stepped into someone else's life. Mal had been sprayed by a skunk. These small occurrences set in motion the event that would bring about a big change.

Libby waited in the hall and listened for the jangling of keys as Mal dropped his pants onto the floor, then waited for the bathroom door to close and for the

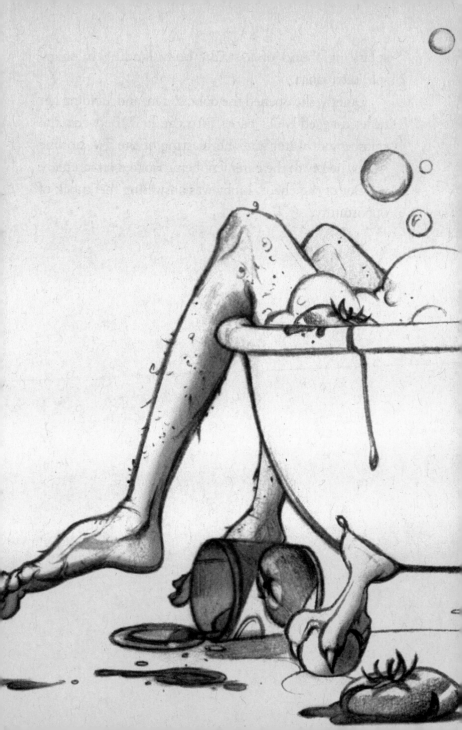

splashing sound of a stinky body landing in soapy spaghetti sauce.

Quietly, she opened the door, slid in, and, holding her nose, dragged Mal's pants into the hall. Between the splashing of water and the blasting of the TV, no one heard the key to the basement being worked off its chain.

Out of the chaos, Libby was answering the knock of opportunity.

Chopped liver

In Eastern philosophy, breathing is the key to enlightenment. For the next half hour, Libby was very unenlightened: She was holding her breath.

She did this because (a) after his bath, Mal had put on the same clothes, so he still stank, and (b) Libby was terrified that he would notice the missing key.

"Libby!" Sal called.

Libby rushed downstairs. "*Queen for Once* is almost on and I don't have my French fries. I also want chopped liver to take away the smell of skunk. Go make some."

"Yes, Mother." Libby had never made chopped liver, but anything covered in maple syrup tasted good to Sal, so she would figure it out.

Libby dumped the fries into the grease. At the very back of the cupboard, she found a can. Most of the label had peeled off, it was so old. All that remained was a corner that showed a picture of a dog with floppy ears. She opened the can. The contents were brown and meaty, and they did look chopped. They also smelled a bit like skunk.

"Libby!" Mal shouted.

Libby held her breath.

"She's making my snack," Sal said.

Libby dumped the meat onto a plate, then covered it with maple syrup.

"Clean the bathtub, Libby," Mal shouted. "Maybe you can reuse the chunks of tomato."

"When are you coming back?" Sal asked.

"After I cheat my clients and find that skunk."

The front door slammed, and finally, Libby breathed. She hadn't yet thought about how she would get the key back *onto* the key chain. If she had, she might not have breathed.

As it turned out, returning the key wasn't an issue.

A hairy orange

Libby placed the food in front of her mother. On the TV was a lady, almost as fat as Sal, walking on a treadmill. By the end of the show, she'd be standing on a cruise ship, wearing a crown and waving at the peasants on the shore.

How nice if Sal could get on that show and have a makeover. Maybe *then* she'd be happy.

Libby waited until Sal's hand began the automatic movement from plate to mouth to make sure the chopped liver was okay.

Then she tiptoed down the stairs to the basement.

Her hands shook as she inserted the key into the lock. Carefully, she turned the key, then twisted the doorknob. It stuck. She jiggled the key a little. The door swung open.

The room was dark. The smell of dust and chemicals floated toward her.

Libby's heart was pounding; she considered running back upstairs. But what she really feared was that there would be nothing interesting in the basement.

She felt along the wall for the light switch and flipped it on. A strange laboratory appeared.

There was a table with three large metal boxes on it. What were they? Across from that were shelves with bottles and jars and curious objects: a plastic eyeball floating in a glass globe, an orange that had grown a head of hair, a cactus dripping a purple substance into a jar, a pair of men's shoes with wings, and a tiny maple tree. There were tubes connected to a bubbling pot, and a large contraption with a metal arm shooting out of it, like the cuckoo on a clock. A sign on it said LIGHTNING ATTRACTOR. Why did Mal need a sign? Didn't *he* know what it was?

Libby was about to examine these treasures when she heard skittering and scattering noises coming from the metal boxes. Were they cages? She froze, then bolted for the stairs. At the bottom, though, she stopped. This was her one and only chance. Mal was sure to notice the missing key.

Besides, whatever was in those boxes was locked inside. Keeping her back to them, she returned to the shelves to read the labels on the jars.

Those on the top shelf seemed to be ingredients: GREEGLE, PETAL POWER, GROUND CRECIO BUGS, CYANIDE, ROSE PETAL WATER, ROSE RED, LOTUS LEAVES, ROSE EXTRACT, EYE OF NEWT (she recognized that from books), COCKROACH TENTACLES, CONCH SHELL OIL, ROTGUT, JEEPERS CREEPERS, MAROONED WHALE, SNAKE OIL, TREE FROG BELLY, CROCODILE TEARS.

The jars on the next shelf had labels in Mal's writing: *Curio Drops, Obedience Ointment, Magnifying Wax, Popple*

Tree Poison, Hypnotic Spray, Metamorphosis, Head Antiache, Telepathy Tapenade, Rose Rot, Hair Today–Gone Tomorrow, Comprehension Cream, Rat Vat, Lifting Soda, Aloe Anguish, Belly Buster.

Libby had just read *Alice's Adventures in Wonderland*, where Alice eats and drinks things that make her bigger or smaller. *What will happen if I try these potions?* she thought.

Not to try *something* would be like looking at the cover of a book without opening it.

She picked up the bottle labeled METAMORPHOSIS. A metamorphosis was a change. But what kind?

She set it back down. OBEDIENCE OINTMENT? That was the last thing she needed.

COMPREHENSION CREAM? Comprehension was understanding. There couldn't be much wrong with that.

She opened the bottle. The cream was purple.

She applied the cream to her hands. Nothing happened. She put a drop of it on her tongue. It tasted bitter. Liberty set down the cream and picked up the bottle of lifting soda.

All of a sudden she heard a mumbling sound, like a news station. She shoved the bottle into her big pocket. She turned. The boxes were indeed cages. She was face to face with one of their occupants.

A slithering tree

A chicken stared back at her. It had red and white feathers and tiny black eyes.

At first glance, it appeared normal, even pretty. But then Libby's eyes traveled down to the bottom of the filthy cage.

The chicken had feet—human feet! Libby knew from picture books that chickens had claws. Here, though, were five toes like her own, on the end of a fat foot.

The chicken opened its beak and burped. "Excuse me."

What? she thought.

"Excuse me."

She heard the voice in her mind, but loudly, like spoken words. Libby peered into the cage. Maybe there was something hidden, a radio or a telephone.

Finding nothing, she moved to the next cage. This one was empty, except for some twigs and branches.

But then the branches began to move, to slither toward her. Libby jumped back. A snake's head appeared, its tongue darting out, its skin covered with thorny branches.

As the snake raised its head to peer at her, Libby smelled roses.

Was she imagining it, or did the snake look sad?

The mumble grew clearer. "If you calculate how many steps to the door, the exit would be . . ."

The voice seemed to come from the next cage. This one held two cute guinea pigs, one black and one brown. Nothing unusual about them.

"Hello, little guinea pigs," Libby said.

"Don't call me that." The black one wiggled its whiskers angrily.

Libby's mouth dropped open. "Did you speak to me? Is that possible?"

The black guinea pig stood on its hind legs and gripped the bars of the cage. "I said, don't call me a guinea pig." Its mouth didn't move. Still, she was sure *it* was speaking.

-3 1

"That's what you are. Isn't it?"

"Certainly not. I'm a rat. And so is my brother. The wicked one turned us into guinea pigs. He chopped off our beautiful tails and dipped us in something foul."

Libby didn't think rats' tails were particularly beautiful, but she didn't say so.

"My brother spends all of his time calculating ways to get us out, but it's useless."

Was she dreaming? The only people she had talked to in her life were her parents, and once a school official who came by and asked her if she was learning at home. Her parents' dark glances were enough to make her answer yes.

To have a guinea pig speaking to her was like

something out of a book. Then she remembered Mal saying, "I was making a deal with a skunk."

"Did my father lock you up?"

"Your father?" The brown guinea pig, whom Libby had heard counting, stopped his calculations. "The wicked one is your father?" Both rodents shook in terror. They scurried to the far end of the cage and turned their backs on her.

"Please don't turn away! It's not my fault he's my father."

"Don't worry about them," a low voice said. "They're temperamental and none too bright." Liberty turned to the snake.

The guinea pigs rushed forward. "Who are you to say we're not bright?" Black shouted.

"You're no more than a slithering tree!" Brown added.

"A rosebush, to be precise," said the snake. "And I agree with the girl. It's not her fault that her father is the wicked one. But she can help us."

"How?" Libby asked.

"Open the cages."

Chicken sense

"That's right," Brown shouted. "It's only fifty-two steps to that window. It will take us twenty seconds to climb the wall, then ten to get out."

"Plot their escape," the chicken clucked. "That's all they ever do. Such boring creatures." The chicken had a lovely voice, like a grandmother might have.

"Well, what do *you* do?" asked Black.

"I think," the chicken said, "therefore I am. Without the awareness of your own self, you do not exist. I'm not a farm chicken laying eggs, or a meal for someone's table. I was a pet. I have a name: Mabel. My owner was a famous astronomer. But then he went to Fiji to study the stars from the other side of the world. He wanted to see what they looked like upside down. As soon as he left, his wife sold me for fifty cents to the wicked one, who experimented on me. So here I am in this cage, with human feet of all things. Thank goodness my feathers are so fluffy that I can barely see them."

"We can see them clear enough," said Black.

"And smell them," Brown added.

"Mabel doesn't want to escape," said the snake.

"The world is not much better out there than it is in here," Mabel said.

"The world is a beautiful place," the snake said, "with cool grass, hot sun, flowing rivers, flowers, and breezes. I would shed fifty skins for just one day out there."

"Yes," Black said. "How I long for subway tunnels, trash heaps, city dumps, and sewers."

"There are rabid dogs and butchers." Mabel shuddered, her feathers fluffing up.

You've heard people say that time flies when you're having fun. Libby was so delighted to have company, she didn't notice the time. Luckily, Sal had fallen asleep in her chair. An intelligent, enlightening show had come on and it knocked her right out.

Unluckily, some poor family's house had burned down. Mal was rushing home for his magnifying glass so he could show them the fine print.

"Now that the pleasantries are over, would you kindly release us," Black said to Libby.

Just as she got to know them, they wanted to leave!

"I'll get in trouble," she said. "I'll be punished."

"You're going to leave us in these jail cells?" Brown said.

"You don't understand. . . ." Libby shuddered. She considered all of the punishments Mal could inflict on her. But then she thought of the snake's thorny skin, the chicken's feet, the miserable guinea pig/rats.

This is what is called a crisis of conscience. Libby knew in her heart that she should free the poor creatures, but she was terrified of the consequences. If you are a child facing such a crisis, it helps to talk to a trusted grown-up. Libby, of course, did not know one. She had to decide for herself.

"Hurry up, girl!" Black said.

"I'll do it." She went to the guinea pigs' cage.

"Open the window, too," Brown said. "It won't do us any good to be trapped in here. He'll only catch us again."

Libby unlatched the door of the cage.

"If we were still rats, we could run straight up that wall. As it is . . ."

Libby lifted the guinea pigs and placed them on the windowsill.

-35

She turned to the other cages.

"Don't bother with me. I don't have anywhere to go. Where could I belong looking like this?" Mabel lifted one foot, then the other. "At least the wicked one feeds me."

Libby smiled. There would be one animal left for her.

The front door slammed. The smell of skunk perme-ated the house. Libby's heart jumped. "Hurry!" She opened the snake's cage, grabbed the snake on the un-thorny part, and rushed to the window.

It took all of them to open the window. Brown and Black scurried out at top speed.

"Rats they are," the snake said. "Well, thanks. Have

a good life. Oh, one last thing! The wicked one hides green papers behind the bricks."

"Green papers?"

"Small green papers. They must be important; he counts them and gets very excited."

"Libby!" Mal called. "Where's Libby?"

The snake dropped to the ground and slithered away.

She heard Mal's footsteps and ducked behind the shelves. Mabel tucked her head into her feathers. "Why is the door unlocked?" Mal said. The basement door creaked open.

The smell of skunk filled the air.

Caught

Mal appeared at the bottom of the stairs. In his arms, looking stunned and scared, was a skunk. Libby listened carefully, but the skunk was silent.

"The light on." Mal surveyed his laboratory. "A draft. The window!" Mal ran to the cages. "My creatures! Where are my creatures? My snake! My guinea pigs! Years of work. Years!"

Libby began to crawl toward the door. But her movement drew Mal's attention. "You!" His voice was burning ice, if such a thing is possible. He shoved the skunk into a cage. "You let my creatures out!"

Libby leapt to her feet. For the first time ever, she spoke back to her father. "What right do you have to turn rats into guinea pigs?"

"How do you know that? Have you been spying on me?"

"*They* told me, that's how. And what are you going to do to that poor skunk?"

Mal's eyes got wide. "*They* told you? What have you been using?" He turned to his potions.

Libby seized the chance and ran for the stairs.

"Stop! Get back here right now. Traitor! I'll teach you

a lesson. I'll turn you into a reptile. I'll make hair grow on your tongue. I'll lock you in a cage. I'll give you a stomachache that will last forever!" Libby heard a cracking noise as Mal's head hit the doorframe at the top of the stairs.

Libby dashed through the hall, but then she made a mistake. Out of habit, she ran out the back door instead of the front.

The concrete walls made the yard into a prison.

Mal rushed out after her, his forehead dripping blood, his mouth foaming with rage. "I'll punish you!"

Sal appeared in the doorway. "Now, Mal . . . she's just a child. Whatever she did can't be *that* bad."

"Shut up!"

As Sal tried to follow, she got stuck in the doorway. "Mal! I'm stuck."

"Who cares." Mal moved toward Libby. "I've got you now."

Libby looked at the concrete walls covered with vines so thick they seemed to choke the house. All of a sudden, she remembered "Jack and the Beanstalk." She leapt onto the vines and began to climb.

"Where do you think you're going?" Mal chased after her. "The roof? And what will you do from there?"

"Be careful, Libby!" Sal shrieked.

"What about me?" Mal snapped. "Don't you want *me* to be careful?"

At the top, Libby climbed onto the roof and ran. In

only a second, she reached the end of it. There was no place else to go.

Mal's bleeding head appeared, then his ugly skinny neck. He crawled behind her on his hands and knees, clutching the roof tiles.

If you've ever had a day where everything seems lost, you will understand how Libby felt.

Mal would reach her. He would lock her in a cage and experiment upon her. It made the idea of putting her hands in toilets sound like a holiday.

I'll jump, she thought. *I don't care what happens at the bottom.* But as she looked down, her eyes fell on the bottle in her pocket.

She took it out and held it up.

Mal froze in horror. "My lifting soda."

"If you come closer, I'll pour it out." Libby unscrewed the cap.

"Don't you dare!" He came toward her, but slower than before.

"I'll smash it to the ground."

Mal froze again. "Have you forgotten I'm your father?"

"*You've* forgotten," she shouted. She had never shouted before. It made her feel powerful.

"Now, Libby, dear. Give us our soda. It took years to distill that. It's very special and we mustn't pour it out. All's forgiven. No worries. I was a bit angry, but now I'm fine. Just. Don't. Pour. Out. My. Soda!"

She was about to dump it, but then she'd have

nothing. Besides, if the comprehension cream made her understand animals, what would this do? She put the bottle to her lips and took a sip. Delicious. Peaches and honey. He was stupid to be hoarding it. He could make a fortune selling the soda just for its taste.

"Don't drink! I've already processed the order for that!" *So he did sell it.* Mal lunged, and wrapped his hand around Libby's ankle.

She kicked at him. His hand slipped. And in that moment, something remarkable happened. Libby began to lift, to levitate, to rise into the air.

She capped the bottle and shoved it back in her pocket.

Straight up she went, higher and higher.

Beneath her, Mal was jumping up and down on the roof, screaming and waving his arms. Above her, the clouds formed a welcoming committee.

An amazing thought came to her.

It was something she had never considered, in her ten years.

Mal had been right. All this time.

He *was* a friggin' genius.

Flying high

Below her, on Gooch Street, Libby could see kids riding bicycles and playing in yards. The houses, aside from theirs, were brightly painted, the lawns green. There were swing sets, gardens, even a couple of swimming pools.

Mal was still waving his arms. Libby couldn't help laughing, although she also felt sad. Her father was her enemy.

The only other person to notice her flight was the man across the street. He waved something happily. It took Liberty a minute to figure out what it was: a long, wiggling worm.

Within minutes, *everything* looked insectlike. Mal was a cockroach with scrambling legs. Sal, still stuck in the doorway, was a fat caterpillar.

Libby kept rising. The sky was a beautiful place, with changing colors. Life now felt like that sky.

Around her, she heard music. It was as if the clouds had strings—cellos and harps—and the breeze sounded through a flute. Was it possible she could comprehend nature as well?

Her whole life she had wanted escape and adventure, and now here it was.

Am I dreaming? She wondered what Sal would think about her floating away. Sal had tried to protect her, had asked Mal to leave her be, had said that morning she should have a childhood. The thought made Libby feel warm inside, like when she was offered ice cream. Was it being married to Mal that ruined Sal's life, like she always said? Had Mal ruined Sal?

A white cloud parted for her like a doorway.

Remember what I said earlier about time? Libby had been rising for five minutes, but it felt like hours. And in that time, she began to consider her future. She would not go home again, so where *should* she go?

That was the one small hitch in her escape—what to do next. In books, something usually appeared: a gingerbread house, a prince, a garden through a keyhole.

I'll go to boarding school. The Sullivan School. I just need to figure out how to get there, she thought.

Like an answer, the wind picked up, sweeping her east. That was an improvement. She couldn't rise forever. She'd end up right out of this galaxy.

Soon she began to make out shapes, like shadowy pipes reaching into the sky.

* * *

It may seem far-fetched to have a girl floating in the sky, but remember that for most of history, people would have thought that airplanes, electricity, computers, and cell phones were far-fetched.

In this world, anything is possible.

The jet set

Libby drifted lower, like a seagull floating on a current of air, moving toward the shadows. As she got closer, she realized that the shapes were the buildings of the big city. She knew about it from hearing Mal talk and from seeing the news the few times Mal watched TV.

Now she was level with the buildings. It was surprising that no one spotted the unidentified flying object that was Libby, but people in cities with tall buildings are not in the habit of looking up. Living under those looming shapes, they forget there's a sky at all.

If I'm not careful, I'll crash! She dodged an antenna on the top of a tower.

A tall brick building raced toward her. She thought of sipping from the bottle again to rise above it, but then she noticed a clothesline with a row of pigeons perched on it. Throwing out her hands, she caught the line. A flurry of birds erupted. Her body swung forward. She heard the shattering of glass as her foot hit a window. The rope burned her palms.

She hung there a moment, stunned,

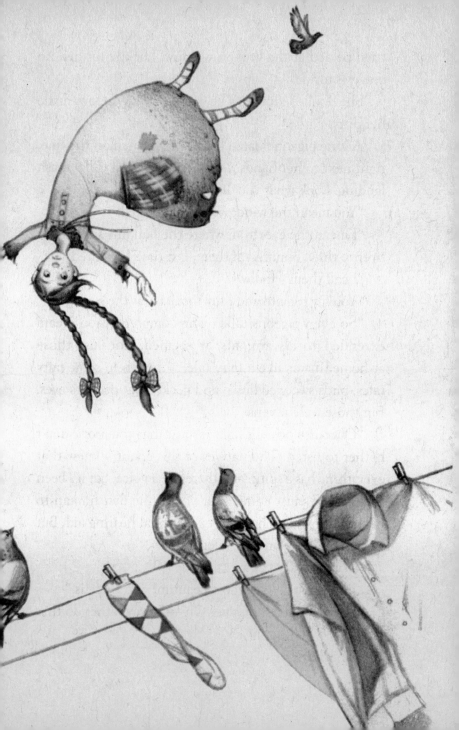

then peered at the broken window. Luckily for her, no one was inside.

She looked down. The street so far below made her dizzy.

A lone pigeon floated back and alighted on the line, right next to her hands. "Now, that's what I call a crash landing. Look what you did to the building's eye!"

"You mean the window?" Liberty asked.

"I mean the eye, from where the building sees. It has twenty-three hundred of them, last time I counted."

"I call them windows."

"You say tomato and I say to*mah*to, as the song goes."

"So even pigeons talk." The comprehension cream extended to all animals, it seemed, not just those at home. It was like a fairy tale, although in some fairy tales, birds swooped down and pecked out people's eyes. But those were ravens.

"Of course pigeons talk. It's just that you *people* don't bother to listen. The natives of this country knew that everything has a spirit, and therefore a voice, but it's been forgotten. I must admit that you're the first human to hear me. *You* must have an exceptional hearing aid. But to which pigeon are you referring?"

"Well, *you*."

"I'm a blue jay, the most beautiful bird there is."

"But . . . you're not *blue*. Oh—did my father do that to you?"

"Do what?"

"Change you from a blue jay into a pigeon."

"Are you from outer space? A pigeon can't change into a blue jay. I am a blue jay, born and raised, and a fine artist. See the white splatters all over that building? Those are mine. I call it *Snowstorm in Spring*."

"What were those other birds on the line?" Liberty asked, suspicious.

"*They* are pigeons. Scavengers. Still, I hang out with them. I'm not sure why."

Libby's body was tingling and felt heavier. Her arms began to tire. Was the lifting fluid wearing off? "Do you, by any chance, know where the Sullivan School is?"

"A pigeon would know. They are excellent at navigation. But you scared them all away."

"Maybe I should just climb in through that window," Liberty mused. "Flying is fun, but you don't have much control."

"You can't do that."

"Why not?"

"Have you heard of the jet set?"

"No."

"The jet set are the rich and famous. They live in that building. Look at your clothes. And those things coming out of your head. What are those?"

"Braids."

"Pardon me for saying so, but you don't belong in that building. Try the one across the way. You'll fit in better.

Just cross right over the clothes. They don't have a brain in their threads, so they won't mind."

Libby began to pull herself along the rope toward the open window across the way.

"What's your name?" the bird called after her. "In case we meet again."

Libby, she started to say, but then she paused. It wasn't her real name, and it no longer suited her; she'd flown away, escaped. "Liberty!"

"My name is Truant. But friends call me Birdbrain . . . the highest of compliments."

Peeping Tom

Hand over hand, Liberty made her way past a pair of polka-dotted pajamas, some socks, and a pretty pink dress. Someday, she would wear colors: sky and flower, leaf and grass colors. Never gray again.

She had almost reached the open window when a head popped out. A woman with black spiky hair glared at her. "Ahhh! A Peeping Tom! A Peeping Tomasina. Call the police!"

Liberty didn't know what a Peeping Tomasina was, but clearly it was not good. "I'm not one of those things."

"Then who are you?"

Liberty racked her brain. A *flying salesman*, she thought. Then she remembered a Curious George book where George washes windows. "I'm a window washer." She felt a twinge of guilt. Lying was what Mal did, not her.

"Where's your bucket?"

"Um, I forgot it?"

"I'll get you a bucket!" The woman ducked back inside.

"Excuse me," Liberty called after her. "Could I come in for a second?" She felt heavier still. What should she do? If the lifting soda wore off, she would crash to the ground.

The woman returned to the window. "Here's your bucket!" She threw a bucket of water on Liberty.

Liberty's wet hands slipped off the rope.

Luckily, the lifting soda hadn't worn off completely. She drifted slowly toward the ground.

As she got lower, people began to notice her. Two children pointed. A street sweeper leaned his head so far back that his hat dropped off.

Liberty tried to land, but each time her feet touched the ground, she lifted again, so that she resembled a ball bouncing down the street.

And as she bounced, she looked around at the city, the world! There was so much to take in. It wasn't like a book, where you might slow down and reread a passage. Marvelous things passed by every second: a woman walking seven dogs of all shapes and sizes, two identical girls who were eating tall ice cream cones, a statue of a naked lady bathing in a fountain, a red two-story bus, shops with windows full of colorful things!

She bounced into a field where children ran back and forth kicking a ball. "Get it," a boy shouted to her. "Kick it!"

With a swift kick, Liberty's foot connected with the

ball. This was another way in which she lived up to her name: She had terrific *aim*. The ball flew at top speed down the field. "Goal!" someone shouted. The team cheered.

What fun! She chased the ball as best she could.

"Wrong way!" the kids who had cheered her shouted. A girl grabbed her by the shoulders and turned her. Again she kicked the ball far down the field. It got close to the net, then a boy shot it in. "Goal!"

A wind swept up, and she began to bounce away.

"Don't go!" Kids chased her. "You're our star player."

She bounced across the street. A truck swerved to avoid her. Cars honked.

The city was built along a river. The bank was lined with trees whose branches swept low like the arms of farmers sowing seeds.

I'd better catch hold of one of those branches, Liberty thought, *before I end up in the water.*

She reached her hands out as she had with the clothesline, but she was out of beginner's luck. She missed the branch by an inch and hit the tree.

Two things happened at once. Her feet sank into the muddy bank and she came to a stop. A large object fell from the tree. Liberty reached out and caught it.

Nine lies

It was a cat, clinging to her for dear life. It had marmalade fur and huge green eyes. "I thought I was a goner," it said.

"A goner?"

"Done. Dead. Finito."

"I read that cats have *nine* lives," Liberty said.

"That was a typographical error in the history books. What cats have are nine *lies*. In ancient days, cats could trick anyone with their lies. Who do you think told Brutus to betray Caesar?"

"I don't know."

"A cat. Who tricked Cleopatra into using a poisonous asp?"

"A cat?"

"You learn quickly. Then, in Rome, the sorceress Thea put a spell on cats to limit their ability to deceive. If they exceeded nine lies, terrible things happened."

"Like what?"

"Fleas, ear mites, and hair balls the size of Texas."

"Really?" Liberty stroked his soft orange fur.

"A bit of an exaggeration. But big enough to choke off their meow! Then there was an era, which I call the

Ignoramus Period, where cats were thought to bring bad luck. I'm a bit of a historian."

"Have *you* run out of lies?"

The cat gave a cat smile. "Years ago."

A low moaning sounded. "Waaaa."

Liberty glanced around to see who was crying, but the only people in the park were far away, flying a kite. She pulled her feet slowly from the mud. It seemed the lifting soda had finally worn off. *I'd better be careful with that stuff*, she thought. *Flying is fun, but there's no control.*

A red bird darted down from the branches. "Can't catch me! Can't catch me!" it taunted the cat, then flew away.

"That nasty bird lured me out onto a weak branch. When you shook the tree, it snapped, and down I came," the cat said. "Never trust a cardinal. That goes for both kinds."

"Both kinds?"

"The bird kind and the church kind. I used to live in the church. The priest made me a nice place under the altar and I slept all through services and never made a peep. But the cardinal came and said it was a sacrilege. Do you know what that is?"

"No."

"Neither do I. But it can't be good, because I was put out."

"Waaaa."

"Do you hear that?" Liberty asked.

"It's the tree. It's a weeping willow, so it cries. It does get old."

"Does it ever speak?"

"Nature doesn't speak. It makes music. The banyan tree twangs. Grass hums. Lilies chime. Dogwood trees bark. Clouds sound like harps, which is why humans associate that music with heaven."

"I never knew that."

"How strange that you understand *me*. You must be the first intelligent human I've met, although you, like the others, use only two legs when you could use four."

Liberty explained about the comprehension cream. "I'm afraid it will wear off. The lifting soda did, although I still have more of that in my pocket." She tapped her pocket to make sure the bottle was still there. "I don't suppose you know where the Sullivan School is?"

"I know where Peggy's Pet-Training School is. I've flunked out of there twice. Too much individuality, they told me. But no Sullivan School. You might ask someone in town."

"I guess it's worth a try."

"What's your name?" the cat asked.

"Liberty Aimes. What's yours?"

"No name."

"Everyone should have a name."

"That *is* my name. No is my first name and Name is my last. The priest named me. His housekeeper had other names for me, but they don't bear repeating in polite company. She's as bad as the cardinal."

"Waaaaa!"

"I wish I could make it feel better," Liberty said.

"It's the tree's destiny to weep, just like it's mine to be a homeless historian. What's your destiny?"

"I'm not sure," Liberty said.

"Better figure it out. Otherwise, you're like a blind man walking through a forest of moving trees."

Street smarts

A chill settled over the warm day. A ribbon of purple rose on the horizon. "Evening already," Liberty said.

"Yes, that tends to happen right on schedule. About forty minutes until it gets dark. You may set me down now. I have to find my supper."

There was something eerie about the coming darkness that gave Liberty a bad feeling. Reluctantly, she placed the soft cat on the ground. "What will I do?"

"You might check the library for the location of the school. I'll show you the way."

Liberty followed No Name through the grass and onto the sidewalk. They walked past a dress shop, a glassblower's, a pet store, a movie theater. Each store seemed a universe to Liberty. "I wonder why some animals talk and others don't. That little dog was simply barking. And those parakeets were just chirping."

"It's a mystery," No Name said. "But I think there must be the *will* to speak. Like every person could learn to play an instrument or paint pictures, but very few bother. People could be kind and good, but most are just worried about themselves."

"You are so wise."

"Yes, I am."

"You know what my destiny might be?" Liberty said.

"What?"

"Liberty. Like my name."

"I'd trade my liberty any day for a warm bed and hot meal. I guess one person's destiny is another's bad luck."

"Warm bed. I have no idea where I'll sleep tonight."

"You can sleep in the church. The pews are hard, but at least you'll have a roof over your head. You'll have to wait until services are over, though."

They turned a corner and entered the heart of the city. Liberty didn't know it, but work was just getting out. She also didn't realize how strange she looked: a muddy girl with long braids in a wet old-fashioned dress.

Amid the bustle were food sellers: a stand with roasted nuts, a coffee stand, a man pushing a hot-dog cart. The smell of the hot dogs reminded Liberty of Sal, of the hours she'd spent in the kitchen preparing food for her mother. It gave her such a mixed feeling of love and fear that she stopped in her tracks.

"What is it?" No Name asked.

"Nothing. I'm just hungry." Although she could speak to the cat just with thoughts, she said it aloud.

Immediately, a woman stopped. She wore a long black coat and sparkly earrings. "Oh, you poor thing. You're hungry. Do you have a home?"

"The Sullivan School," Liberty said. "I'm just on my way."

The woman gave Liberty a strange look. "Don't they wear uniforms there?"

"Tell her it's in the laundry," No Name said.

"It's in the laundry."

"I don't believe a word of it. Well, never mind." The woman took a bill out of her wallet and handed it to Liberty. "Buy yourself some food."

"Thank you!" Liberty called after her.

Another cart moved by. "Apples! Ripe and red." The smell made her mouth water.

"Excuse me," Liberty said. "May I have two apples?"

The man looked her up and down. "What have you got to pay with?"

Liberty showed him the money.

"That'll buy you ten apples."

"But I only want two."

"Suit yourself." The man grabbed the bill out of Liberty's hand and gave her two apples. Then he disappeared into the crowd like a stone thrown in water.

Liberty stared at her empty hand. "I don't get it. If my money bought ten apples, why did he take all of it for two?"

"Not all humans are to be trusted. Take my word for it."

"I believe you." Liberty had hoped that everyone would be wonderful in the world. But it seemed some were good and some were bad, like in fairy tales. How to figure out which was which? "Here, No Name. Have an apple."

"I'd rather my meals have fur on them."

Liberty ate the first apple in no time and started on the second. The food at home always came frozen or in cans or jars. "Delicious."

"You'll have to finish it before you go into the library. We're here."

The book museum

"So that's a library!" Liberty gasped. "It's beautiful."

The city library *was* a magnificent place (add one letter to *place* and you have *palace*), like a museum for books. There were grand white columns, marble stairs, and statues flanking the huge doors.

"I prefer small libraries with shabby carpets and piles of cushions where a cat can curl up and take a good nap. They won't let me set foot in here," No Name said.

"Will you wait for me?" Liberty asked.

"Certainly." No Name yawned. "I'll have a catnap under that flying horse statue. Just find the librarian and ask for directions to the school."

The entrance was marble. Beautiful paintings graced the walls.

More important, there was a sign for something that Liberty needed quite a lot: RESTROOMS.

What a civilized place, Liberty thought, as she ducked into a room with not only bathroom stalls but two stuffed chairs and a vase of flowers. The world was a wonder, no doubt.

She emerged to the sound of a bell chiming three times and the lights blinking on and off. "The library will close in ten minutes," announced a voice over a speaker.

I'd better hurry, Liberty thought. But it was hard to rush, for she had made another discovery about the comprehension cream. She could hear *books*. As she passed the shelves, the words within floated out.

It was the best of times, it was the worst of times. . . .

Anyone lived in a pretty how town. . . .

Far away, where the gray water meets the blue sky . . .

Books are made from trees (even the pages are called leaves). You could say that books are the memories of trees. Combined with ink, the author's dreams, and the reader's imagination, they evolve into forests without limits, and those forests were talking to Liberty!

She saw a woman in a pink blouse standing behind a desk that said REFERENCE. She was young, with curly hair and a very red nose. "Could you please tell me how to get to the Sullivan School?" Liberty asked.

The librarian looked down, and what she saw startled her: a thin girl in a muddy dress, with her hands over her ears.

On another day, the librarian might have questioned her. *Where are your parents? Why do you appear to be wet? Do you have a ride home? What is your favorite book? Why are you covering your ears like you're in pain?*

If the answers hadn't suited her, she might have called Social Services to make sure the girl was okay.

On this day, though, the librarian had a terrible cold. She had sneezed twenty-six times in the last half hour.

That was the bad news. The good news was that a friend had seen the librarian's boyfriend in a jewelry shop asking about engagement rings. Her boyfriend had told the librarian he had a special question to ask at dinner. She was due to meet him at the restaurant in ten minutes. She was in a big rush to get there.

You see, *everyone* has a story.

To know someone's story is to understand them. Once you know the dragon has a bellyache, his habit of breathing fire is more explicable. When you see the ogre's sad,

-65

decrepit house, his bad mood makes sense. Once you understand the librarian's cold and her forthcoming marriage proposal, she can be forgiven for not bundling the poor girl into her car and driving her home.

"One moment." The librarian's name was Margaret Parson, but when she married she would become Margaret Squelch. You can't win them all.

Margaret knew that the Sullivan School was one of the fanciest boarding schools around.

She grabbed a telephone book. "The address is 451 Cherrywood Street in Fairhaven. That's about sixteen miles from here."

Sixteen miles?

"Would you like a map?" Margaret asked.

"Yes, please."

Margaret printed a map and highlighted the path with a bright yellow marker. "Here you are. Good luck."

It was that easy, Liberty thought. *If you want to know something, go to a library.*

The friggin' genius

Curiosity is not limited to cats and Liberty. *You* might also be curious about what was happening on Gooch Street as Liberty floated off to the big city.

At any time in history, gazillions of lives are being lived simultaneously. In Zimbabwe, Thailand, Tasmania, and Borneo, in the poorest hovel and the richest palace, in the sky and on the moon, the lives of ants, plants, gorillas, and people are going on. But we are generally fixated on that infinitesimal thing in the scope of the universe, ourselves.

Evening had come upon Gooch Street and Sal was still stuck in the doorway, sobbing because her daughter was gone, hollering because instead of prying her loose, Mal had climbed over the top of her by stepping on her shoulders and dashed out the front door.

She would, in fact, be there all night. Luckily, the weather was mild. From where she stood, she could still see the TV. She didn't suffer *too* much.

Mal, meanwhile, was running up and down Gooch Street, clutching his head, spreading skunk odor, and gazing into the sky, from where he expected Libby to crash to earth at any moment. He had tested the lifting soda on his animals, allowing them to hover against the ceiling. He knew that its effects did not last very long.

What he didn't know was how high it might take her. His fear was that she would fly out of the galaxy and he would never get his bottle of lifting soda back.

It wasn't that Mal didn't have the recipe. He did; it was on page twelve in his secret recipe book. But the rare Micronesian miniature peach tree that contained the essential oil took twelve years to grow, and had recently died.

A secondary concern was that if Libby landed in the city, she might tell someone about his experiments. Then the animal rights people would descend on his house with their megaphones and news crews.

He did not worry about Libby. He never had. You can't make a pie out of rotten apples.

Finally, Mal took a deep breath and stopped pacing. *I'm a friggin' genius*, he thought. *I can solve anything.* Ignoring his wife's shrieks for help, he returned to his laboratory.

First, he checked on the skunk. The hypnotic spray and rose rot had begun to take effect. The skunk was subdued.

Next, he slathered his hands with comprehension cream and lifted the chicken out of the cage. "All right, you ugly, stupid creature. Tell me exactly what happened this morning."

Mabel was no dummy, however. She shifted from foot to human foot and said nothing.

"Spit it out or I'll teach you a lesson. What did she try, aside from comprehension cream? What did you beasts tell her?"

Mabel fluffed up her feathers.

"She's my daughter," Mal coaxed. "I own her. I have a right to know."

Mabel thought about Liberty, how impressive it was that a fine, brave person was the progeny of such a complete schmuck as Mal.

"I demand an answer!" Mal shook his fist.

Mabel looked the bad apple straight in the eye. She formed three perfect words that were communicated straight into his brain:

Cluck. Cluck. Cluck.

Worm Man again

Speaking of chickens: As Mal was running back and forth outside, like the proverbial chicken with its head cut off, he had an audience. Worm Man watched from behind a fig tree in his garden.

What is happening over there? he wondered. Mal Aimes, who generally only came and left, was running in front of the house. The girl had floated off the roof. It was like a marvelous painting by Chagall (who painted many people flying over towns). Meanwhile, someone inside was screaming up a hullabaloo.

Could it be *her*? Sally Mason?

What if she comes out? He had been waiting years for this to happen so that he could casually walk across the street and talk with her once again.

Worm Man was an oligochaetologist (try to say that three times very quickly), one who studies worms. His particular focus was the earthworm.

He picked up his *Lumbricus terrestris*, also known as the night crawler, which can burrow as deep as eight feet into the ground, then set it back down in the garden. He was observing the shedding of its castings, the process that brings nourishment to soil. (He had originally studied snakes, but the act of feeding the snakes live mice was too repellant. Worm Man himself was a vegetarian. He greatly admired the way the worms ate dead matter, leaves, and trash, harming nothing to keep alive, but adding nutrients and oxygen to the soil.)

He couldn't concentrate. His mind kept wandering to Sally Mason, now known as Sal Aimes.

He had known her his whole life. She was the girl with whom he'd pressed fall leaves into waxed paper, sledded in winter, picked flowers in the spring, sat on porch swings in the summer, and whose Saint Bernard puppy they had trained together.

She had never shared his interest in worms, but she had listened when he told her that to know the life of a worm was to understand the story of all species, their development over time.

Of course, as all people do, they grew up. The night after they graduated from high school, he invited Sally to the lemonade social. They held hands as the mayor gave a speech about how they were now on the journey to adulthood. It was a path with lots of twists and turns, but very exciting. Worm Man (whose real name was Edgar Kind) had a vision of a road filled with travels and scientific adventures. Walking alongside him on this road was none other than Sally Mason.

A week after graduation, though, a tall, skinny man arrived at 33 Gooch Street selling insurance. The man knocked with such persistence that the door finally opened.

Edgar had watched Mal Aimes approach the house.

The skinny man had given him the creeps. He saw Mal duck into the doorway and enter the house, clutching his briefcase.

Mal didn't come back out again. Sally's mother had always been timid and fearful, so Edgar guessed insurance would've appealed to her.

The last time Edgar talked to Sally, she told him she was engaged to Mal. He was one of the richest men in the country, she said, and she was now going to live like a queen and travel the world with him.

Edgar had pretended to be happy for her.

The life Mal had promised Sally was like most of the contracts he offered to his customers, only this one was in words, not writing. Even if she'd had a magnifying glass, she couldn't have read the fine print.

The word around town was that Mal was a pauper who had *wormed* his way into their home (Edgar winced at that expression, naturally), then sold Sally's parents so much insurance, they eventually had to give him the deed to the house. After that, Mal sent them away to live in a retirement home in the South. As far as Edgar knew, Sally's parents had never returned, not even for a visit.

Edgar never saw Sally again, though he knocked on the door many times. He didn't know that Mal had convinced Sally of the catastrophes that would befall her if she answered. Or that Mal, as clever as he was, manufactured fake newspaper articles about the wretched villains and horrible crimes that had become common in their town. He showed them to Sal to scare her out of her wits and to convince her not to leave the house.

Edgar had sent social workers, lawyers, and once even the police to check that Sally was okay. Each time he was told that the newly married couple was fine and well fed (a comment he found odd, since Sally was a twig of a girl). He should mind his own business.

A NO TRESPASSING sign was put up. Worm Man accepted an invitation to go to Fiji to study the *Megascolides australis*, a giant worm that creates massive lemon-shaped cocoons. He traveled to Italy to excavate worm fossils from the volcanic remains of Vesuvius, then on to Ukraine. Worm Man became a world traveler, but he kept his house on Gooch Street.

-73

And every time he came home, he worked on a special project. He had removed part of a wall from his basement. Using his *Lumbricus terrestris* to lead the way, Worm Man and his legion of worms were digging a tunnel under the street. He carefully shoveled behind them.

It was slow work, but they were under the sidewalk in front of 33 Gooch Street.

If the front door wasn't being opened when he knocked, he would go in through the wall of the basement.

Worm Man didn't know about Liberty's existence for a long time.

Then one day, when he was building a snowman, her small dark face appeared in the window. It was like seeing a ghost. *Sally?* he wondered. But Sally couldn't be that young.

The face appeared with more frequency. He might be planting his spring bulbs, making a snowman, or building an arbor, and he'd see her.

That was the girl who had flown off the roof.

He was going over the whole story in his mind, trying to make sense of it, when Mal disappeared into the house.

He watched the door, praying that, miraculously, Sally Mason would appear.

After two hours, the door opened again. Mal came back out. This time he had a skunk on his shoulder. He was staggering under the weight of what looked like a pile of signs.

Edgar wasn't sure what to make of that, but he felt one thing, deep inside him. He was getting closer . . . closer to seeing Sally Mason once again.

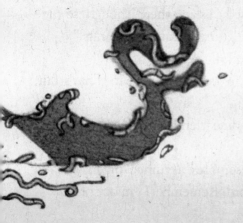

Prayer

Liberty followed No Name to the church. Compared with the library it was small, built with shiny stones that rose out of the ground as naturally as a mountain, and its windows had colorful pictures made of glass.

"It's beautiful," Liberty said.

"I guess." No Name yawned.

"Isn't it locked up at night?"

"The church is always open for those who want to pray. You're not supposed to sleep there, though, so hide if anyone comes in. I'm going to catch some rats."

"You're not going to kill them?"

"I won't kill any I'm not going to eat. That's fair, isn't it?"

"It's just . . . I have some friends who are rats, but they look like guinea pigs."

"Anything that resembles a guinea pig, I'll leave alone. You have my word. Remember? I'm out of lies."

"Okay."

"Don't worry. Most of the time, I have to settle for trash from the Chinese restaurant. I'll see you in the morning."

"I'm so happy you're my friend."

"Likewise." No Name gave his cat smile.

The church was lit by candles. Liberty stretched out on a pew in the back, where it was darkest. She stared at the lovely windows.

If anything is ever going to bug you, worries or fears, it will happen at night when you're trying to sleep.

As Liberty lay there, cold and hungry, the elation of her journey drained away and she began to worry. Would she find the Sullivan School? How would she get food? She doubted that she could just stand on the street and say she was hungry, and have people hand her money.

What happened after she left? Had Mal punished the chicken? She should've taken it with her, but, of course, she hadn't known she was going anywhere. What did Sal do? Did she get unstuck? Who would fry Sal's clams? Would she ever see her mother again?

Tears poured down her cheeks, but she didn't want to wet the bench. Ever since using the comprehension cream, she felt like she understood *objects* better, too, even though they didn't talk. She imagined what it would be like to be a bench and have people sitting and climbing on you all day.

The church door creaked open. Liberty heard footsteps. She peeked over the bench and saw a woman kneel a few rows ahead, her head bowed.

"God," the woman said loudly, "I have some favors to ask. First, I need your help with my shop. The candy is sticking together in the jars. It's eating away my profits. My chocolates are melting. I need air-conditioning. Also, there's the gravity issue. My cakes are falling."

Some people live their lives with a sense of gratitude. Others are never satisfied and constantly complain. This one was a real whiner.

"Third, my husband decided to become a magician. He bought a tuxedo and some rabbits. He keeps making things disappear: the kettle, the telephone, the money I keep in a jar."

The woman went on and on. It was to this comforting sound that Liberty fell asleep.

The drawers of the mind

Liberty had a funny way of thinking about her mind. She imagined it as a room walled with drawers. Open a drawer and there were ideas, thoughts, memories, and other surprising things.

In sleep, many drawers opened at once. She dreamed of the guinea pigs, and of a talking toaster. She dreamed she was on the edge of a vat of hot oil with Mal trying to push her in. Liberty tried to run, but Sal was stuck in the doorway, blocking the exit. As Liberty approached her mother, beseeching her to move, Sal opened her mouth and out floated a lovely song.

Liberty woke up with a start, the image of her mother fresh in her mind.

I miss her, Liberty thought. *But why?*

The question reopened the dream drawer, and out came a song: Sal holding her on her lap and singing, *Baby fishing for a star, fishing near and far*. Sal rocking her and tickling her chin, her voice sweet and clear.

Books, as I said, are the memories of trees. But dreams are the memories of time.

Could it be? Was her mother once nice?

Liberty sat up. Light poured in colors through the stained glass.

The door of the church creaked open. Liberty knelt the way the lady had, her head bowed. It gave her a peaceful feeling.

When she glanced up, she saw a man wearing long robes, lighting the candles.

A moment later, No Name appeared, smelling like Chinese food. Liberty tiptoed out after him.

The city was bathed in blue light. The buildings cast shadows across the empty streets.

It was a magical feeling, to be awake while most of the world slept. *Even better,* she thought, *to be part of it. And free!*

She could walk down the street, talk to whomever she wanted, go inside shops (although she didn't have money to buy anything).

"How did you sleep?" No Name licked sticky sauce from his fur.

"Okay. Did you get to sleep in the priest's house?"

"No. He had friends for dinner. Every time I snuck in, one of them, a *lady,* pretended that I made her sneeze. They put me out, so I hit the trash bins in Chinatown. I'll never eat another egg roll as long as I live."

Liberty's stomach groaned. She'd eat an egg roll, whatever that was.

"Oh, and guess what?" No Name said.

"What?"

"You're famous." No Name stopped on a street corner and looked up. Nailed to a telephone pole was an enormous sign made out of poster board.

LOST: OUR BELOVED CHILD
LIBBY AIMES
$10,000 REWARD FOR HER RETURN
NO QUESTIONS ASKED
CALL 799-0065

Liberty didn't remember her parents taking a picture of her, but there it was, a huge photograph, her braids hanging down like two ropes waiting to be climbed.

They had never had a phone at home. Mal always said they couldn't afford it. But he had a cell phone for work that he kept in his pocket. He was fond of saying, "Call me on my cell phone if you need anything." It was like reading the fine print. Since they didn't have a phone at home, they couldn't call him when he was gone.

"These signs weren't out here last night," No Name said, "so whoever put them up . . ."

"My dad."

". . . must be around."

Liberty heard footsteps. She turned with a start, expecting to see Mal's nasty face, his mustache like the bristles of a filthy toothbrush above his lip. But it was just a man rushing along with his briefcase.

Liberty pulled the map out of her pocket. "I'd better find the school. Will you come with me?"

"If schools are anything like libraries, stores, and restaurants," No Name said, "I won't be allowed in."

The pleasure with which Liberty had greeted the day melted. Tears, once again, rose into her eyes. "I'll miss you."

"Don't cry. We'll meet again. If you find a place where cats are allowed, come and find me at the church. Remember, it's on the corner of George Street and Washington Avenue."

Liberty looked up at the street signs and at the sign with her own face. "You're the best friend I ever had." She picked up No Name and cuddled him.

"One word of advice for you," No Name purred.

"Yes."

"Stay away from scoundrels."

"What's a scoundrel?"

"A person who enjoys bringing misery to others. A villain."

"Oh." Most books had a villain. "How will I tell which ones are scoundrels?"

"That's the tricky part." No Name leapt from her arms. He rubbed against her legs, purring, then dashed off down the street.

Free food

Now the city was waking up. Doors opened. People jogged by. Cars began to crowd the streets, their radios blasting the morning news through open windows.

Liberty checked her map. Her hands shook from fear that Mal was nearby. Her legs wobbled from hunger like overcooked noodles. She'd never been much for eating because the food she cooked for Sal was greasy and disgusting, even when it *wasn't* covered in maple syrup. Liberty had not tasted ripe cherries, or a fresh salad with chopped herbs, crunchy carrots, and sweet tomatoes. The food at home was either frozen or canned. Still, she had eaten a bit at every meal. She'd never experienced hunger.

Worse, as the doors of the cafés swung open for business, the scent of breakfast floated in the air: baked sweets, coffee, hot chocolate, and eggs and bacon.

Then there were the sights: street stands with mountains of colorful fruits, windows displaying cheeses and meats. She had to remind herself that she was in a hurry, in danger, so that she didn't stop and ogle every single display.

* * *

As Liberty walked, she looked to the left and right, behind her and in front of her for Mal. She passed an art gallery, a French restaurant, and a shop that seemed to contain anything you might put in your mouth, ears, or eyes: toothbrushes and toothpaste, chewing gum, mints, toothpicks, dental floss, penny candy that actually cost a dime, eyedrops, eyeglasses, sunglasses, contact lenses and contact lens solution, nose spray, nose drops, cotton swabs, and medicine for stuffy noses. She longed to go and pick up every item; they were all so colorful. She passed a shop with a dazzling array of shoes. How would those colorful shoes look with her shabby gray dress?

A man with a top hat was painting a sign that said MAGIC STORE. On a hunch, Liberty looked in that shop's window. Sure enough, the woman from the church was chasing a bunch of white rabbits around with a broom. Suddenly, the woman dashed out the door and swept her broom right at her husband's head, knocking off his hat. A few white rabbits escaped onto the street. Liberty would've stopped to chat with them if she weren't so afraid of being caught by Mal.

She turned a corner onto an even busier street. *Better to be lost in a crowd.* She stopped to gaze into a window filled with chocolate cakes, pastries, tarts, and cookies. It was more enticing than even the gingerbread house in "Hansel and Gretel." In the window was a sign: FREE SAMPLE.

She went inside. There was a woman and a man, as round as her mother, wearing a white apron and a tall white hat.

On top of the counter was a plate with little lacy cups. Each cup had a piece of yellow cake topped with pink frosting. Shyly, Liberty took one and began to eat. It was delicious.

She reached for another.

"One per customer," the woman snapped.

Liberty pulled back her hand. There was so much she didn't know about the world and how to be in it.

"She can have another, Velma," the man in the apron said. "Can't you see our little friend is hungry? And how about a nice cup of coffee. On me." He poured a cup of coffee, loaded it with sugar and cream, then grabbed a doughnut from a tray and plopped it into a bag. "Here you go. Breakfast."

It was the first meal anyone had made for *her*.

"Thank you!" Mal had always insisted on manners. She had to thank him each morning for their house, for the food she got to cook, for each time he *allowed* her to cut his toenails. At any rate, manners were the one useful thing Mal had given her, despite the circumstances.

"She's been in here before, taking free samples." The woman narrowed her eyes.

"No she hasn't," the man said. "I'd remember *her*."

"Her face is so familiar. Where have I seen you?"

Had the woman seen the poster? "I'd better go." Liberty dashed outside.

The streets were now filled with people on their way to work. Liberty walked among them eating her doughnut and drinking the sweet coffee. If it weren't for Mal's signs, she would've felt so happy among the people and the world, so full of wonder.

She joined a crowd crossing the street, stepping around workmen who were climbing out of a hole in the ground.

Suddenly, through the crowd, she saw the words SULLIVAN SCHOOL. The words were moving at a good clip, appearing and disappearing. Liberty had to push her way through the crowd to chase after them.

SULLIVAN SCHOOL. There they were again. Printed in blue letters across the back of two sweatshirts.

The sweatshirts turned a corner. "Sullivan School!" Liberty called, chasing after them, stepping into the street to go faster. A yellow car marked TAXICAB honked loudly. *Those cars are everywhere*, Liberty thought. They sure honked more than other cars.

Liberty had almost reached them, two girls walking arm in arm.

But then she smelled a skunk.

A moment later, she saw Mal, rushing among the people, his greasy head swiveling to and fro above the crowd.

It almost made her giggle, to see what an odd picture Mal made, like a giraffe among a flock of sheep.

But this was no time to laugh; the next second, his telescope head turned and he looked straight at her. "Libby!" He began shoving people. "Out of my way! That's my daughter!"

Liberty turned and ran. She ran in front of the honking taxis, crossing the street. She turned the corner, then dashed into an apartment building with a revolving door. She leapt out of the moving door into the lobby.

The walls inside were mirrored. The floors were marble, like the library's floors.

She flattened herself against the wall as she'd seen a character do on one of Sal's TV shows.

A man wearing a red jacket and cap stood behind a little stand. "Pretending to be wallpaper?" he asked.

"Uh-huh," Liberty answered. "I mean . . . I'm just waiting for my mother."

The man came over. He had bushy eyebrows that practically covered his eyes. "Are you saying that you and your mother live here?"

"No."

"I didn't think so. I know everyone who lives here."

"We're just visiting someone."

"Whom are you visiting?"

Liberty peeked out. She couldn't see Mal. "I think maybe I'm in the wrong building."

The man bent toward her. "Why, you're the girl on the sign!"

"There's my mother!" Liberty shoved past him and out the door.

Mal was now crossing the street. Under his arm was the skunk!

Liberty thought fast. She could drink the lifting soda and fly away, but who knew where that would take her? She could run as fast as she could in the opposite direction. She could hide. The playground equipment in the park had places where she might not be seen. There was a tube and a big slide with a house on top of it. Near the workmen there was a giant crane. She could climb to the top of it.

A crowd had collected on the corner, waiting for the light. Liberty slid in among them, and ducked until the light changed.

As she crossed the street, she noticed the workmen were loading their equipment onto a truck.

-89

While their backs were turned, Liberty went under the yellow tape and dashed to the manhole.

Unlike the rabbit hole that led to Wonderland, this one had a ladder. Lowering herself in, she climbed down rung by rung.

The ground was slimy under her worn shoes. Rats scrambled over her feet. None of them spoke.

She stood paralyzed in the shaft of light from the hole, her hand still on the last rung of the ladder.

The sewer smelled like the world's busiest bathroom.

She thought about Mal's plan to lower her into the sewers to work.

Now here she was after all: Alice in Wasteland.

Down the rabbit hole

Liberty heard voices above her. "Youz guys up for the game, then?"

"Yep. I got the chips and beer." The man burped. The other laughed.

"Let's call it a day."

A moment later, the heavy lid was pushed over the hole.

She was in total darkness.

Without anything to distract the eyes, the mind tends to go a bit wild. It's why most people are afraid of the dark. This happened to Liberty.

Will I ever get out of here? Even if I do, I'll never escape him, Liberty thought. *Mal has signs everywhere and he's a friggin' genius.* The image from her nightmare popped into her mind: Mal with a ferret head pushing her into a vat of hot oil. *What if he really does cook me in a vat of hot oil? No, that was just a dream. Still, he's sure to catch me. I'll never make it to boarding school.*

Uncertainty, having grabbed her mind like a dog latching onto a bone, would not let go. In the dark, tears streamed down her face. *And when I return to my life, it will be worse than ever, because now I know how it feels to walk down the street, to go to a library, to pet a cat.*

I will let you in on a secret. Having a heartfelt cry is like putting helium into a balloon. Your spirits will lift much faster than if you just ignore your misery.

After ten minutes of sobbing, Liberty began to feel better and recover her strength. *Well, I can't just stand here. I'm facing the direction I was supposed to, to go toward the school. I might as well start walking.*

Carefully, she made her way through the dark, slimy tunnel, sliding one hand along the wall for guidance. She could hear the street sounds above, which comforted her.

The sewer did not just have rats. It also had giant cockroaches, which skittered over Liberty's hand. And each time, without fail, she gasped in horror. After one particularly gruesome encounter with the giant insects, she let out a scream.

"Shut up, will you?" a voice said.

Liberty looked around, her eyes finally settling on a dim vision at her feet, a white rat with trembling whiskers. "Sorry," she said. "One of those . . . giant insects ran across my hand and it startled me."

"Cockroach!"

"Excuse me?"

"It was a cockroach. The lowest creatures on earth. And people think it's *us*. You're a big rat. I'll bet you're greedy to have grown so large."

"I'm not a rat," Liberty said, offended.

"You speak rat. Skidmore is a skinny rat because of greedy, giant rats like you."

"Who's Skidmore?"

"Me. That's who."

"Well, I'm a person, Skidmore. Can't you tell?"

"Everyone's saying they're something different than what they are. It's like living with a bunch of politicians. Rats saying they're people. Guinea pigs saying they're rats."

"Guinea pigs?"

"Biggest complainers I ever met. 'At our house, we got to eat fried clams. At our house, we had a warm cage.' "

"That's them!"

"Worse, they had a snake with them. Very unpopular. It ate a couple of my friends."

"Where are they?"

"We told them to get lost, so they moved to California. At least, the guinea pigs did. They had a plan to get shipped with some food. Pretty smart, they were. Click and Clack, they called themselves. One of 'em was a whiz at math. Had all the calculations." Skidmore raised up on his back legs.

"Oh."

"So if you're not a rat, maybe you eat rats?"

"I hardly think so."

"Skidmore will put up a fight."

Liberty sighed. "Can you tell me how to get out of here?"

"Why should I?"

"So I won't eat you," Liberty said, as fiercely as she could.

Skidmore trembled. "The only way out is up. You have to find the light."

Liberty looked up and all around. Darkness.

"But be careful. If you pop up in the wrong place, a car might drive over your tail. That happened to my cousin. Can I go now?"

"You could've gone all along. You're certainly faster than I am."

"Skidmore escapes by his wits once more." The rat dashed off.

Alone again, Liberty continued her sad walk through the sewer under the city. It would've been nice to meet up with the guinea pigs. The song that Sal had sung came once again into her mind. She pretended the song was dancing ahead of her, like the Pied Piper, that she could follow it out of the sewer. *Baby fishing for a star* . . . Another memory came. Sitting on the rug playing with blocks. They were colorful, even though the paint was chipped, and she and Sal were stacking them. Where were those blocks now?

The city sounds had disappeared, Liberty noticed. The muck around her feet was getting deeper. How long had she been here? She couldn't tell.

Her mind shifted to all of the stories she'd read, but she couldn't think of any where someone got out of a *hole*. The characters were stuck in other ways: Rapunzel in her tower, Sleeping Beauty in her glass coffin, the frog in his bog. Always, it seemed, there was someone else to help out. Except for Alice; she just woke up from a dream.

Fishing near and far. She was so absorbed in the stories and the song in her mind that at first she didn't notice. Light. Two small streams of light pouring from above.

She felt along the wall for the ladder.

But there was none. No way out.

Out of the frying pan

Here's where it could get really adventurous. The water rises and she can't get out. She gets washed into the sea. Or she spends years making footholds in the wall with a pebble. When she finally escapes she is eighty, too old to go to boarding school. Instead, she goes to an old people's home, and pretends it is boarding school.

But what actually happened was simple. Not finding the ladder, Liberty reached into her pocket and drew out the lifting soda.

This time, she didn't swallow. She just touched the rim of the bottle with her tongue.

It took longer than she remembered for the soda to work. She rose a foot off the ground. Another touch with her tongue and she rose to the top. After capping the bottle, she shoved it back into her deep pocket.

The manhole cover was heavy. She had to push and shove, using pressure from her own rising body. Finally she worked the cover to the side.

Liberty held tight to the edge of the hole so she wouldn't fly away. Then she waited for the lifting soda to wear off, ducking whenever cars drove by. *I don't want to*

lose my tail, she joked silently (she was in a much better mood now that she was back in light and sunshine).

When her arms grew heavy, she pulled herself onto the street. She was no longer in the city. She could see its tall buildings in the distance, but around her was a quiet neighborhood. There were houses larger than she could have imagined behind gates and stone walls, and gardens. They made her think of the house across the street at 34 Gooch, and of how much she had always longed to enter its beautiful garden. Worm Man, as her mother had called him, was always doing something fun and interesting in his garden: tending plants, making an arbor, building a snowman, harvesting his small vegetable crops, picking plums from his tree. A pang of homesickness shot through her. *But home is a prison*, she reminded herself.

Still feeling light and bouncy, Liberty went to the sidewalk and searched for signs with her picture. There were none. At least that was something to be happy about. She had managed to escape Mal.

"Dear Mother," a voice said, "sorry I took so long to write. I don't like to write, which is why it took so long."

Liberty looked around.

"Dear Walter, be advised that hereafter I no longer want to be called Pooky, but my real name: Gloria."

She followed the voices to a big blue box on the sidewalk. Liberty went closer, half expecting a person to step out. MAIL PICKUP: 4:00, it said on the box. The mail at 33 Gooch came through a slot on the door. Here, it seemed, was a big box for *everybody's* mail.

"Dear Sarina, your love is like a red, red rose."

"Dear Customer, thank you for your note. As far as a refund . . . fat chance."

Apparently, she could hear the mail as well as books.

She took out her map and studied it, then looked at the street signs. None of them corresponded to the map. The river was nowhere in sight. She had no idea where she was.

It was baking hot, that part of the day when people are at work and at school, and the world seems sleepy. And hungry. Lunch hour was fast approaching, and Liberty's stomach growled furiously. *Even fried clams sound good right now*, she thought.

A splat of white goop hit the ground in front of her. She looked up as a bird zoomed down. Instinctively, she ducked.

"Circle of life." The bird landed at her feet and nodded to its splotch.

"Birdbrain!" She put out her arm. Birdbrain hopped up. "How good to see you!"

"You won't believe what happened," Birdbrain said. "After I talked to you, I went to my therapy session. I've been going forever, with no improvement to my bad mood."

"You did seem a bit ill-tempered," Liberty admitted.

"I talked about my childhood and blah blah blah. But then . . . you won't believe what the therapist said."

"What?"

"He said, 'We pigeons have a need for community. It's part of us. You've been spending too much time alone.' Can you believe it?"

"What?"

"You were right! I *am* a pigeon. No one ever told me that before."

"You're kidding?"

"See, I was raised by blue jays after my mother had an unfortunate encounter with a Mack truck. That much I knew. But no one ever told me she was a pigeon."

"Really?"

"A bona fide pigeon. I've always hung around pigeons, but I felt like a loser for doing so." Birdbrain made sobbing sounds. "Now I can finally be happy."

"It must be hard to not be who you think you are."

"It was. And I owe you an apology. It was rude of me to say you're not a member of the jet set. It's the heart that really matters, not how you look."

"That's okay." Liberty smiled. "Since you're a pigeon now, maybe you can help me find my way."

"Of course."

Liberty showed Birdbrain the map. "See, there's the river. And that's the Sullivan School. It's right on the river, but on the other side."

"Gee . . . I'm new at this navigation stuff. Not so sure. But I can probably find it using my aerial skills. I had those even as a blue jay."

"That would help."

"Wait here. I'll locate it, then I'll take you. But I can't get too close to the river. I'm very afraid of water. It's one reason I've never seen my reflection."

"You must *drink* water," Liberty said.

"But only from little shallow puddles. If I'd seen my reflection, I would have never thought myself a blue jay." Birdbrain soared away.

As Liberty waited for him to return, she looked at the houses in wonder. Inside were families. She wished she could join one. She thought again of Sal, sitting on the floor with building blocks. Maybe her mother could come with her.

With a great flapping of wings, Birdbrain returned. "I found the river. It's just a couple of blocks from here."

As Liberty followed Birdbrain, who darted up and down (more like a mockingbird than a pigeon), the neighborhood fell away and the streets became busier. They passed a post office, a school, and a little market with a fruit stand outside that made Liberty's mouth water.

She kept her eyes open for signs and for Mal. Thank goodness he was so tall and stood out so much.

Along the way, Birdbrain made art, splattering the sidewalk and parked cars. Liberty wondered how he had so much in him.

Birdbrain alighted on her shoulder. She hoped he wouldn't drop anything there, but was too polite to say so. "Well, kiddo," he said. "There she is. Just ahead of us. Water."

"I have to get to the other side somehow."

"Maybe if I keep up with my therapy, I'll be brave enough to fly over it one day. That would be fun."

"I hate to say goodbye."

"Me too." Birdbrain pecked her ear affectionately. "Maybe we'll see each other again sometime. Look at all the statues in the park. I'm going to decorate that one. I'll call it *Horse Waiting for Rain*. See you at the Sullivan School someday!" Birdbrain soared across the park, landing on a statue of a man astride a horse.

Lunch hour had arrived. The park along the water was filled with people eating out of sacks, walking, strolling babies, and picnicking. How Liberty longed to be part of that world, better than any fairy tale.

She sniffed the air for any hint of skunk. But all she smelled was the sweetness of the cherry blossoms (and heard their bell-like sound).

She walked down the bank, splashed herself with water, and tried to wash the muck off her shoes.

Thank goodness I'm out of that tunnel, she thought. *Nothing could be much worse than that.*

Have you ever heard the saying *Out of the frying pan, into the fire?* What it means is that you have left a bad situation, only to enter a more difficult one.

Into the fire

Liberty peered once again at her map. No matter how hard she tried, she couldn't figure out the distance to the dot that the librarian had marked as the Sullivan School, or how she could cross the river.

"Yoo-hoo, little girl." A woman tapped her shoulder. She had long golden hair, like a fairy-tale princess, and wore a pink ruffled dress. Next to her stood a man, also attractive, but oddly dressed in pants so short that his hairy ankles stuck out, and wearing two different shoes. "Will you please snap our photo?"

The man held out a camera. "The light is perfect."

Liberty stepped back. "I don't know how to use a camera."

"It's easy," the woman cooed. "You just look through the hole and push the button."

The man pressed the camera on her. Liberty had no choice but to take it.

The couple stepped back. Liberty looked through the camera. The couple hugged and smiled hugely. *Click.*

"Now we'll take one of you," the woman said.

"No." Liberty handed back the camera. "I have to go."

"Where are you off to in such a pretty dress?" the woman asked. "A party? A dance class?"

Liberty's stomach felt funny, like when Mal came home. She was *not* wearing a pretty dress. The woman was lying. "To school."

"Which school, may I ask?"

You may not, Liberty wanted to say. "The Sullivan School."

"Oh," the woman gushed, "what a fine school. My cousin went there when she was younger. It's on the other side of the river, you know, about twelve miles from here. Surely you're not going to walk?"

She really does know where it is, Liberty thought. "I'm . . . getting a ride. You can cross the river walking, can't you?"

-103

"No," the man said.

"If you don't want to wait for your ride, we'd be happy to drop you off. We pass by there on our way home," the woman said.

Liberty frowned. She had an uneasy feeling, but twelve miles . . . that *was* far. It would be the middle of the night when she arrived. And in a car, she would be safe from Mal.

"We insist," the man said. "You can call your ride from my phone and tell them not to bother."

The woman took her arm. "My name is Lola Garden and this is my husband, Albert. Now you know our names. It's like we're old friends."

Liberty was glad they didn't ask for *her* name. Lying gave her a bad feeling.

Between us, they didn't ask her name because they already knew it.

One of the first lessons good parents teach their children is not to get into cars with strangers. Liberty, as we know, did not have good parents.

She was uneasy as she slid into the backseat. What if they saw the signs on the way? What would they do? What if they took her to the wrong place?

She worried even more when Albert, instead of getting into the front, slid in beside her.

Lola locked the doors and screeched away, cackling hysterically.

Albert shoved Liberty down and tied her hands behind her back. "Stay down. We don't want anyone seeing you."

"Not until we get our ten thousand dollars," Lola added.

In less time than it takes to say "out of the frying pan," Liberty was in the fire.

Scoundrels

Liberty tried to keep track of the direction of the car as it sped and turned. "Are you taking me to the Sullivan School?" she asked, even though she knew there was no chance of that.

"Gag her." Lola's sweet voice had soured.

Albert took a handkerchief out of his pocket. "Don't worry," he whispered. "I've never blown my nose on this. I just have it to be gentlemanly."

Liberty didn't think it was too gentlemanly to stuff it in her mouth, but since she was gagged, she couldn't say so.

"Call the number," Lola commanded.

"What number?" Albert asked.

"The number from the sign, the one I told you to write down."

"Oops."

"Scoundrel! Didn't you write down the number?"

A *scoundrel*, like No Name had said. A *villain*.

"Now I have to go back and find another sign." Lola zipped the car around.

"Could you stop making those turns so fast?" Albert begged. "I'm going to vomit."

Even worse, Liberty thought, *a vomiting villain.*

Splat. A white blob hit the windshield. *Splat.*

"What is with that pigeon?" Lola said. "It keeps pooping on the windshield."

Birdbrain! Somehow, he would help her.

"There's a sign. Give me the phone." Lola swerved to a stop. She started to get out of the car, but then ducked back in. "That pigeon is attacking me!"

Birdbrain! Liberty called out in her mind.

But Birdbrain must've been too far away to hear her.

She tried to sit up, but Albert held her in place. "Don't make Lola mad," he said. "She's got a wicked temper."

You're no picnic, either, she wanted to tell him.

"I can see the sign from here if I just pull forward," Lola said. *Splat.* She turned on the windshield wipers. Water sprayed out, destroying Birdbrain's art.

The car sped away again. "I've entered the number into the phone," Lola said. "Call and tell them we've got her and to bring the ten thousand dollars to our hideaway."

Albert took the phone. "There's no answer."

"Leave a message."

"Hello, we have apprehended Libby Aimes and will be trading her for the exact reward. Call us at 224-1960. Faster." Albert hung up. "I'm afraid of birds. Did you ever see that movie where they peck out everyone's eyes?"

"I can't speed. Do you want the police after us?" Lola

said. "With a kidnapped child! You know what will happen if we have to face Judge Hardnose again?"

"Don't say that name," Albert whined.

"Judge Hardnose. Judge Hardnose. Honest, upright, goody-two-shoes Judge Hardnose at the district court. If we meet up with him again, it will be curtains for us."

"Just curtains?" Albert said. "That's not too bad. Especially on a bright day when I've had too much beer the night before. If the sun comes through, it hurts my head."

"I mean jail!"

"Oh." He gulped. "There's the turn to the bridge."

The car swerved again. The streetlamps and telephone poles disappeared and there was just sky. Liberty's heart sank. They were going over water. Birdbrain would not follow.

"At least that bird has stopped poop-bombing us," Lola said. "Why haven't they called back?"

"What will we do if they don't?"

"Bump her off, I suppose."

"Bump her—" Albert covered Liberty's ears, but she could hear anyway. "We certainly can't do that. . . ."

Bump her off? Liberty wondered what that meant. It did not sound pleasant.

Love nest

"We're here. Hunky-dory!" The car came to a stop.

"I wish you would not use that phrase," Lola said.

"Hunky-dory. Hunky-dory!"

"Judge Hardnose. Judge Hardnose."

"Truce!" Albert allowed Liberty to sit up.

"I'll fetch some rope from the trash heap and we'll tie her legs," Lola said.

They were in a deserted alleyway, at the back of a dilapidated building. Lola returned with thick rope and tied Liberty's ankles together.

Liberty smelled old trash and rotting fish as she was led from the car. She looked up. Not a bird in the sky. Then she heard voices. She wanted to call out for help, but the gag was still in her mouth. "Bill for heating services: $265. We heat it. You eat it."

"Notice of demolition."

"We should try to burglarize that mailbox when it gets dark," Lola said.

It was only a mailbox.

The door of the building was glass, but it had been smashed. Jagged pieces stuck out. Albert reached his hand inside and unlocked the door.

They walked up three flights of rickety stairs, Liberty tripping on the rope that bound her feet.

"You always find the nicest places for us to stay," Lola said. *"Not!"*

"Can I take the gag out now?" Albert asked when they came to a door. "The building's abandoned, and she doesn't look very comfortable." Albert had a queasy feeling about the whole thing. That was the real reason he felt like vomiting. He had never gotten the hang of enjoying someone else's suffering, like a true scoundrel.

"I don't want to hear the brat prattle on. Give me the key," Lola demanded.

"I think that was a yes." Albert took the gag out of Liberty's mouth.

When Lola flung the door open, they found that the place *was* nice. There was a big red couch, a glass coffee table, and a well-appointed desk and chair. Aside from empty beer bottles scattered around the floor, the room was clean.

"Whose pad is this?" Lola asked.

"Thug used it as a hideaway after he robbed that dance studio."

"It's actually quaint."

"It's our love nest." Albert giggled.

"Look." Lola opened the curtains. "There's a little balcony out here with a table for eating lunch."

"Lunch!" Albert said. "I'm dying of hunger." The phone rang. "Oh my God! What do I say?"

"Just tell them where to meet us and that they have to bring the money."

"Hello? Yes . . . Yes, we have her. Exactly as in the picture. Sort of starved-looking and dirty in a black dress."

"Gray," Lola corrected.

"Uh, gray," he said. "Yes, I'm sure it's her, and if you don't come get her, we'll bump her off."

"Idiot!" Lola knocked the phone out of his hands. "Do you want them to think we're kidnappers?"

"That's what you said in the park, that we'd kidnap her."

She snatched the phone off the floor. "They've hung up."

The phone rang again.

"Hello." Lola used her sweet voice. "Yes, the dear girl is right here. My husband has an odd sense of humor. He thinks his jokes are funny, but nobody else does. We shall take good care of her. My husband will give you the address. Oh, and don't forget the ten thousand dollars. You will not get her back without the dough."

"Dough," Albert moaned. "That reminds me of bread."

"Give him the directions." Lola shoved the phone into his hand.

Liberty listened as Albert read the directions, but nothing corresponded to her map. Except, they *were* across the river.

Albert hung up. "He's coming from the suburbs, so it

will take an hour. Ten thousand dollars will be ours, and everything will be hunky-dory!"

I can't believe it, Liberty thought. *I'll be given back to Mal.* She scanned the room. How to escape?

"Don't get smug, Albert," Lola said. "It isn't over until the fat lady sings."

"I don't know any fat ladies, so how can they sing?"

But Liberty knew a fat lady. And at that moment, she wanted her more than anything.

Bad apples

As Liberty was dragged over the river by the two scoundrels, Sal was in a state of confusion. Her daughter had flown off the roof. Her husband had disappeared.

There was no one to cook her meals, but it didn't matter. Sal missed Liberty so much, she wasn't hungry.

Nor could she focus on the TV, whose voices only reminded her that she was alone. Without the TV blasting, she did something she hadn't done in a very long time: She thought.

I should go look for her too, she thought, *but I can't manage out there*. This was something Mal had told her, not only in her waking hours, but also, unbeknownst to her, in her sleep.

For the twelve years they'd been married, he had suggested to Sal day and night that she was incompetent, incapable, stupid, and lame.

Without Mal around to drill this into her head, though, Sal was beginning to have a sliver of doubt.

She stood up, then sat down again.

She thought about the question that nagged her day and night. *Am I a terrible mother?*

An image of Libby came to mind. Her girl. Her daughter. It was that day she was asking to go out, the tears rising in her eyes.

Is she having a terrible childhood?

Certainly, Sal's own childhood had been better than Liberty's. She couldn't deny that. She went to school and to parties. She went to stores, parks, soda fountains, and movies.

Perhaps you've heard this saying: *One bad apple spoils the whole bunch.* It means that a bruised and rotting apple ruins the rest of the apples in the bag or bowl.

Sal had been a happy, albeit shy, girl, prone to fits of giggles and bursts of song. When she had her daughter, she'd delighted in caring for her and teaching her games. After years of being married to a rotten apple, though, she had gradually become one herself.

Furthermore, Mal had convinced her that the world was dangerous. Fear is a powerful tool of control. It was what Mal did for a living. Fear was one reason that now, Sal didn't answer the persistent knock on the front door. *Who could it be?* She sat up and listened. She covered her ears until the knocking stopped. "Who is it?" she finally called out, but, of course, they were gone.

What if it's Libby? But Libby would know I'm not allowed to answer the door. She would come in.

Will I ever see Libby again?

The question was too painful to contemplate. As if her mind were a radio, Sal changed the station and pondered the chicken instead.

It had appeared that morning, after she'd finally escaped the door frame. Clucking, it had teetered across the living room floor, then settled on a patch of carpet. It looked like it would lay an egg any second.

The first thought Sal had was: *FRIED CHICKEN!* One of her favorite foods. But then she remembered that she wasn't hungry anymore, and that she didn't know how to cook, let alone pluck a chicken.

Then she thought, *A mutant chicken from Mars*. It was a rare leap of imagination for Sal, provoked by the sight of the bird's human feet!

She went to the kitchen, got a dish of water and some cornflakes, and sprinkled them on the floor. The chicken stepped awkwardly around on its weird feet, pecking at the cornflakes.

When the chicken was fed, Sal picked it up and put it on her lap.

It was nice, Sal remembered, to have a pet. As a child, she had a dog and a hamster. The dog was her best friend, aside from Edgar Kind.

Sal thought about her own parents. They had been good parents, had seemed to love her *then*. There had been hugs and kisses, family meals, books and toys, homework help—all of the things that make children happy. Yet once they moved to Florida, where Mal convinced them their health would improve, she never heard from them again. Mal said they had moved without even leaving a forwarding address. It was as if, having married her off, they had forgotten her.

What Sal didn't know was that Mal had sent her parents a letter informing them of the house sale. He wrote that he and Sal were moving to Iceland. They would be living beside a volcano, studying its eruptions for the insurance industry. The mail wasn't delivered there because of the molten lava.

Of course, Sal's parents could have hopped on a plane and searched for them. It was something they discussed often. But Sal's mother was a very timid person. That's how Mal had wormed his way (apologies to Worm Man) into their home. Sal's parents were scaredy-cats (apologies to No Name), especially when it came to flying.

But then again, if they had been brave enough to fly to Iceland and pick their way through the

volcano-laden landscape, they would not have found Mal and Sal.

They were never there to begin with.

Sal petted the chicken's soft feathers. "I'm going to see my daughter again," she promised.

Sal could have sworn the chicken was nodding in agreement.

Hunky-dory

Albert and Lola sat on the couch, two bookends wedging Liberty in. All three of them watched the clock.

Liberty was trying to come up with a plan. The only thing she could think of was getting to the balcony, drinking lifting soda, and flying away.

"Why hasn't he come yet?" Albert finally said.

"You said it would take an hour . . . ," Lola said.

Five more minutes passed. Albert twiddled his thumbs. "Why hasn't he come yet? It's been fifteen minutes."

"Will you stop asking that?" Lola snapped.

Albert's stomach growled. "We'll starve to death here."

"We *ate*," Lola said.

"That was yesterday, and it was just ketchup and Tabasco we stole and put in hot water. Cook something, Lola, like a good wifey."

"I don't cook."

"You make me go on all of these . . . capers, and you don't even feed me. My mommy was a wonderful cook. She used to make me happy-face pancakes every morning."

"I'll check the kitchen, but I'm not cooking anything." Lola began opening and closing cupboards. "There's nothing here. Just . . . oatmeal."

"Well, by all means, cook it," Albert said. "It's not much, but it will keep us from perishing."

"I don't cook!" Lola slammed the oatmeal down on the counter.

The story of Goldilocks popped into Liberty's head. This was like that, breaking into someone else's house and eating their porridge. An idea lit up in her mind. "I can cook," Liberty said. "That's my job at home. I do all the cooking."

"But you're tied up," Lola said.

"You'll be surprised how good I can make oatmeal taste. I can make it taste like peaches!"

"What if she poisons the food?" Lola said.

"Where would she get poison? I'll keep her legs tied and I'll watch her like a hawk."

"Oh, very well." Lola sighed. "I am going to the bathroom to wash up for lunch. Don't take your eyes off of her."

"I won't." Albert untied Liberty's hands and led her to the kitchen.

Liberty smiled sweetly at Albert. "Please get me a pan and put a cup of water in it."

"What fun. It's like I'm an assistant chef."

"Now I'll take the oatmeal."

"If I hadn't met Lola, I would still be working for a butcher, pulling the gizzards out of turkeys and stuffing sausages. She convinced me that a life of crime would be easy, but to tell the truth, it's more difficult than just holding a job."

"I can imagine."

"What I really wanted to do was to be a conductor." Albert began humming. He picked up a wooden spoon and pretended to conduct. "How fabulous to stand onstage waving your arms around, with everyone watching. Best of all, you never have to face the audience. All they see is your back."

Liberty poured the oatmeal into the bubbling water. Leaning against the stove, she felt the lifting soda in her pocket. Her idea was to have Albert and Lola float to the ceiling and be trapped. Then she could flee out the door—unless they made her eat first. That would be a problem. "It's almost ready. We'll need bowls and spoons."

"I'm salivating. It smells so good. With the ten thousand dollars we get for you, I'm dining out every night."

Where would Mal get ten thousand dollars? Liberty wondered. He always claimed to be broke. Probably he'd find a way to cheat them. "One more thing. The most important thing," Liberty said. "Sugar."

"But I've checked every cupboard. There was nothing but the oatmeal."

Liberty thought hard. "Sometimes, people store sugar in a desk drawer. To keep it dry. I used to do that at home."

"You're kidding?"

"The moisture in kitchens, what with the steam . . ."

"Oh, very clever. You stay right there. I'm not taking my eyes off of you." Albert walked backward to the desk.

Liberty smiled and nodded, all the while unscrewing the cap in her pocket.

Albert didn't find sugar, but he did find other amusing items that captured his attention. "Hunky-dory! Colored rubber bands." He shoved them in his pocket. "A two-dollar bill. Yippee. A ballpoint pen!"

Liberty was so nervous, she dumped the whole bottle of lifting soda into the pan.

"No sugar." Albert returned with his pockets full. "But money, a bouncy ball, a ballpoint pen, and gum!"

-121

"Lunch is ready."

"It does smell like peaches. I'm practically drooling." He grabbed a spoon. "Just one taste."

"You mustn't do that. It's bad luck to eat before everyone is seated."

"You *are* handy to have around. If he doesn't come to fetch you, we should keep you. Children can get away with crimes that adults can't. I'll bet you could even steal a diamond."

"I'll bet I could," Liberty said.

Albert picked up the bowls. "We'll eat outside on the little balcony."

Liberty was so worried he would begin eating that she called for Lola. "Lunch is served."

Lola came out. "I don't see any lunch."

"We're dining alfresco," Albert said. "That means outdoors."

"I know what it means," Lola snapped. "You need to gag her. We can't have her hollering outside."

"But how will she eat her porridge?"

"She won't. That's the beauty of it. She can see her food, but she won't be able to eat it."

"I insist that she eat."

"Fine. She can eat after, in the bathroom. We can't have her shouting outside. There could be people around."

Lola stuffed the gag in Liberty's mouth and led her to the table. "Come along, you spoiled brat. Ten thousand dollars. No one has ever paid that much for me."

"I would if I had it, darling," Albert said.

"Thank you," Lola said in a sulky voice.

As the two sat in front of their bowls, Liberty felt much like she had after stealing Mal's keys. She wondered about the time. If Mal showed up and found out she'd used the rest of the lifting soda, he'd be sure to teach her the worst lesson in the world.

"I'm so hungry I could vomit." Albert began to eat.

"This oatmeal *looks* like vomit," Lola said.

Liberty peered anxiously at Lola. They needed to both eat at the same time for it to work.

"Mmm. Magical." Albert wolfed down his food. "You *must* try this, Lola."

Albert had almost finished his bowl. But nothing had happened. Had mixing the lifting soda with food altered it?

Lola picked up her spoon. Then she stopped. "Albert, we do not get up from the table during lunch."

Liberty's heart sank. Albert was going to fly but not Lola. She would be stuck with just *her*.

Albert tried to hold on to the table, but it was too late. He floated to the ceiling of the balcony.

"Come back here!" Lola grabbed Albert around the waist.

For a moment, Lola steadied him, but then he began to rise again, taking Lola with him. "This is not an amusing joke, Albert! Jumping into the air with me attached!"

Before Lola could figure out what was going on, Liberty hopped over. "I'll help you!" she said, grabbing Lola's legs and pretending to pull her down. Using all of her strength, Liberty yanked them to the edge of the balcony and shoved them off. "Hang on tight, Lola!"

"Yippee!" Albert shouted as the pair were swept off the balcony into the sky.

"I'll get you for this, Libby Aimes!" Lola screamed.

Two ropes

Liberty wanted to watch, but she knew she didn't have much time. She rushed inside and checked the clock. Fifteen minutes before Mal would arrive! She was about to run out the door, but then she stopped.

She drank a glass of water and used the bathroom. Looking in the mirror, she thought about the photo that led the scoundrels to her.

She found scissors. Her braids were a part of her, like her fingers and toes. She shuddered as she sheared off each one, leaving them on the floor like discarded ropes. She searched the closets for a change of clothes, but they were empty, aside from a huge pile of ballet shoes. Then she remembered: The apartment's owner had burglarized a dance studio.

She ran into the living room. Anything else she needed to do?

Inspiration is a fine thing when out of thin air, ideas float forth. I'd like to say that inspiration is unique to humans, but anyone who has seen a dog jump on the couch when it thinks no one is looking or a horse leap over its fence and tear off through a field knows otherwise.

At any rate, looking around the room, Liberty had an inspiration.

She rushed to the desk and grabbed a piece of paper and a pen.

Dear Judge Hardnose, she wrote in her neatest printing,

> At 33 Gooch St. lives a man
> named Mal Aimes. For years, he
> has cheated his customers by
> selling insurance policies with fine
> print at the bottom that makes
> them useless. He is a crook.

She sealed the letter and put a stamp on it. She didn't have an address, so she just wrote in large letters on the front: JUDGE HARDNOSE. DISTRICT COURT.

She wrote the city and state. URGENT, she added at the bottom.

She put the pen in her pocket. *This will be helpful to mark my map.*

Liberty grabbed the letter and tiptoed down the stairs. She looked in every direction before leaving the building; then she dropped her letter in the mailbox.

The streets were empty. She had no idea where she was. But one thing she did know. The Sullivan School was on this side of the river.

The other thing she knew was that Mal was coming. She didn't think he had a car. But there was so much she didn't know about him. His whole life was a secret. She wished she'd find out he wasn't really her father. Her real father would be a prince in a far-off land, or even a friendly woodcutter. Did they still have those around these days?

Liberty searched the birds in the sky, looking for Birdbrain, but they were all seagulls, hovering over the town dump.

Just as she turned into an alley, she heard a car screech to a halt on the street behind her. Liberty crawled through the alley, only standing when she had turned the corner. She listened; the car door slammed so hard, she knew it had to be Mal. She took off running.

The secret was to stay hidden and try to find her way back to the river, for the school was nestled near it, according to her map.

She dashed between buildings, peering around corners, so that she resembled an actor in a spy movie.

After an hour, she still hadn't found the river or any streets that corresponded to her map. Hungry and exhausted, she was about to give up when a strange sight appeared: a giant bicycle with only one wheel and an orange seat big enough for three people. The rider was carrying a huge burlap sack of something lumpy.

Liberty had learned her lesson about strangers, but she had not been taught about staring. As the boy rode past her, she gazed at him in wonderment.

When he saw that he had an audience, he rode in circles around her, stopped, started, and spun on his wheel in a way that was marvelous, all while balancing the large sack.

Liberty couldn't help but smile. The cyclist, too old to be a boy but too young to be a grown-up, hopped off the bike and bowed.

Since he was right in front of her, Liberty decided to take her chances. She pulled out her map. "Do you know the way to the Sullivan School?"

The boy scratched his head, peered at the map, burst into a huge smile, and nodded. Then he gestured to the one-wheeled thing. She was to get on.

"I'll walk. I just need to know the direction, and how far I should go."

His fingers formed an inch, but then he spread his arms to indicate farther. He bowed and gestured again.

What should I do? Liberty thought. *He seems to be offering me a ride. But how can I trust him? How can I trust anyone?*

This seemed to be the most important question in life. Whom to trust? Which were the scoundrels, which weren't? It is actually one of the most important things we *all* must learn.

No Name had helped her. So had the librarian. Birdbrain had been trustworthy, although he had seemed a bit obnoxious at first.

But Albert and Lola . . . she'd had a funny feeling in her stomach when the couple approached, a twisting, a foreboding.

The young man hopped onto his one-wheeled bike with his burlap sack and rode in front of her, indicating she should climb onto a bench and then hop on behind him.

As she looked at the young man, Liberty's stomach did not twist or turn. It felt perfectly calm, although hungry.

She climbed onto the bench and jumped on, holding on to his waist for dear life as they zipped off at full speed.

This one-wheeled bike was like a magic carpet ride. It was as much fun as flying, only they were still on the ground.

At one point, when they leapt off a curb, he dropped his sack. Out rolled a few potatoes. He and Liberty got off and collected them. Then the young man juggled the potatoes as they went, Liberty holding on tightly.

After about an hour, the river appeared. *We must be close now,* Liberty thought. The young man pulled up in front of a massive green tent and gestured for her to get off. Then he tipped his cap and, still juggling, sped off before she could even thank him.

Is this the Sullivan School? Liberty gazed around.

It looked nothing like the brochure.

There was a reason for that.

Godwin the Terrible

Liberty peered around her. She couldn't see an entrance. But as she walked around the tent, she found a gap and slid through it.

Inside was a big stage with three small circles marked off. Surrounding it were stadium seats. Above, a long rope was suspended across the tent, and a giant swing hung from it. On the ground were more one-wheeled bicycles, juggling pins, hoops, and balls.

What fun, Liberty thought, and she began looking around. She thought she would climb up the ladder and try the swing. But on the way she saw a large cage. A sign said GODWIN THE TERRIBLE. Inside was a lion.

"Hello!" She went over to the cage.

The lion roared, displaying razor-sharp teeth.

"Can you understand me?"

The lion roared again. This time Liberty could hear faint words beneath the roar. "I'm bored."

"You must be, in that cage," Liberty said.

"You can speak Lion?"

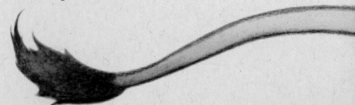

Quickly, Liberty told him about Mal's lab and the comprehension cream.

"That's a good story," the lion said. "I'm not as bored. If you tell me more stories, I might let you tame me."

"You seem pretty tame."

"Do you want to pet me?"

Liberty reached in and stroked the lion's soft mane.

"It's you! The Amazing Madame Torso!" A man rushed up to her. "Exactly on time. I can hardly believe my eyes. And you've already tamed Godwin the Terrible." The man wore green tights and a short black jacket. He had a thin waxed mustache that grew all the way to his knees. "I didn't think you'd be so small, so youthful. That face cream you sell must work wonders. Already, I can see you perform miracles. Our last tamer, Snap, never *patted* Godwin. He poked him with a chair. I'm sure you're famished, Madame Torso. We'll dine, and I'll introduce you to everyone."

The word "dine" kept Liberty from admitting that she was not Madame Torso. "Hello."

The man bowed. "Modesto Impregno, as you know. So happy to meet you at last. I fed Godwin this morning in preparation for your arrival."

"Don't interrupt my story time!" Godwin roared angrily.

"That's no way to greet your new tamer, Godwin. I must apologize for him. Times, as I mentioned in my letter, have been hard. Godwin has not been able to have the amount of meat he is used to. To tell the truth, all he's been eating is soup, hot dogs, and the occasional squirrel. It's made him a little, uh, disgruntled. But in your correspondence, you said you could tame *any* lion."

"Come inside my cage," Godwin said. "We'll show him. I won't eat you. I promise."

Liberty was suspicious, but having a meal did seem to relate to taming the lion. "Can I go in the cage?" she asked Modesto.

"Of course! But let me get you your whip and chair. The show is tonight, so there's no time to lose."

"My whip?"

"Unless you've brought your own. You seem to have come without luggage."

"No. I don't have my own."

Modesto dashed off.

"Are you going to whip me?" Godwin asked.

"Certainly not."

"Come in. Tell me a story."

She slid the heavy bolt across, opened the cage door, slipped in, and bolted the door shut.

"Once upon a time . . . ," she began. Liberty's mind, dizzy with hunger, was not as quick as usual. Otherwise, she might have used a story she'd read, like "Hansel and Gretel." Instead, she tried to make one up.

"Once upon a time . . ."

"I heard that part already."

Just then Liberty noticed that at the back of Godwin's cage was a large mirror. It gave her an idea.

". . . there was a city made of mirrors. The buildings were mirrors. The streets were mirrors."

"Scratch behind my ears." The lion's fur smelled like sawdust.

"And when the sun moved in the sky, the mirrors lit up with beautiful colors. At first, the world worked well, but then people became so dazzled by the sight of their own reflections, they stopped talking to one another. They spoke only to themselves, saying how beautiful they were."

"That's what happens when I look in my mirror. I am so dazzled by my reflection that nothing else interests me."

"So the world was rebuilt, this time with glass. People watched each other instead of themselves. Only, everyone found out things that they shouldn't know, like who argued and who was messy." *This is pretty fun*, Liberty thought.

"Where are the lions?"

"The lions?"

"Yes, it's people this and people that." Godwin yawned.

"Okay," Liberty said. "I'll start over. Once upon a time, there was a lion named . . ."

"Godwin."

"That's right. Godwin lived in a city of mirrors. Everywhere he looked, he saw his own reflection."

"I love it!"

"Madame Torso!" Modesto returned with the chair and whip. "What they say is true. You are amazing!"

And where was the real Amazing Madame Torso, you might wonder? She was thirty miles away, but being quite ancient and old-fashioned, she preferred to travel by stagecoach. Stagecoaches, as you know, are often held up by bandits. That was the case here. Bandits had demanded her jewels, her costumes, and the boxes of her famous wrinkle cream.

She pretended to reach for her jewels, but instead grabbed her whip, cracked it, and lassoed each bandit, yanking them from their bicycles (they were too poor to have horses). At the moment she was tying them to the coach to bring them to the proper authorities.

Everyone has a story. Especially Madame Torso. They don't call her Amazing for nothing.

Potatoes

Liberty followed Modesto out of the tent and into a trailer, where three people were already eating: a man wearing a clown suit and a giant orange wig, a woman in pink tights and a red corset, and, much to her delight, the young man from the one-wheeled cycle, who jumped up and clapped his hands.

"This is Jordan, our helper."

Modesto pointed to the young man. "He doesn't speak. He only emotes. He does odds and ends here, like shopping, feeding the animals, and cleaning." Jordan did a backflip. "This is Carl, our clown; and Vrushenka, our acrobat, tightrope walker, and resident cynic."

"What is a cynic?" Liberty asked.

"A pessimist. One who believes that the worst is around the corner."

"Is not around corner." Vrushenka had an accent. "Is here. Only people too dumb too notice."

"And this, my friends, is the Amazing Madame Torso."

Carl frowned. "But Madame Torso is over a hundred years old."

"Her face cream works wonders," Modesto said.

"This is not Madame Torso," Vrushenka said. "This is little girl. Godwin will eat her in one bite. Then swallow her bones."

"Must you elaborate so, Vrushenka?

If you'll remember, Godwin did not eat the bones of Snap, our dear departed lion tamer. He left those behind, as well as his foot and shoulder. Besides, Madame Torso is experienced. She has already been in the cage."

"Excuse me," Liberty said quietly. "I don't want to disappoint you, but I'm not Madame Torso." She hoped they would let her eat before she had to leave.

"See!" Vrushenka gloated.

"Then who are you?" Modesto rubbed his head.

Liberty thought about the signs all over town with her name on them. "You can call me Alice." It was her way of not lying, but not exactly telling the truth.

"But you *did* tame Godwin, Alice. My eyes weren't deceiving me!" Modesto said.

"Yes, I think I can tame him. But did you just say he ate someone?"

The opposite of a pessimist is an optimist. That is someone who believes everything will work out well in the end, no matter what. Modesto was an optimist. "It was because we were broke and he hadn't been fed. We'll feed him before you enter the cage again. No worries." Modesto clapped his hands. "Well, since Madame Torso did not show up, you're hired! The show opens tonight. And now . . . for the feast!"

"Feast! Ha!" Vrushenka said. "Potato soup morning, noon, and night. In Russia at least we have cabbage and beet soups."

"That is not so," Modesto argued. "We have mashed

potatoes for breakfast, potato soup for lunch, and vichyssoise for dinner."

"Vichyssoise is just cold potato soup," said Carl.

There is something called perspective. What that means is that people see things depending upon their own experiences. You may think you have an ordinary house and a humdrum supper. But if someone arrives who has lived in a mud hut and had only rice each meal, your house will look like a mansion, and your ordinary meal, a feast.

To Liberty, a bowl of potato soup sounded stupendous. She gulped down two bowls of it in no time.

"I suppose you were wondering how we came to be here," Modesto said. Actually, Liberty was marveling at how *she'd* ended up here, but she nodded politely. -139

Modesto stood and bowed. "I was born in the circus. My mother was the famed trapeze artist Altruista Modesto. Her name combines the two most important human qualities: altruism and modesty. One day, when she was swinging on the trapeze, I decided to be born. My father—the ringleader, like I am—caught me."

"Ha!" Vrushenka said. "My life far more interesting. I grew up in Siberia. My father was famous poet, jailed many times for his words. We so poor, he could not afford paper. So he wrote on the walls of apartment. Then we ran out of walls, so we all had to memorize the poems."

"My family was so poor, we had to *eat* our memories," Carl said.

"Always, you one-up me. One-up. One-up." Vrushenka waved him away.

Next Jordan stood up, gesturing wildly. He laughed, then he cried. And then he sat down.

"Jordan's story is mystery," Vrushenka added. "He just arrived one day, like you, and has followed us ever since. Modesto is kindhearted and put him to work."

"Despite our complaining," Modesto said, "we all love the circus. It is our life, like the paints are the artist's life, the laboratory that of the scientist. It is our . . . destiny."

There's that word again, Liberty thought.

Modesto looked at his watch. "Oh dear. Three hours until showtime. We must digest our food—"

"Vat's to digest?" Vrushenka said.

"—get into our costumes, feed the lion, and warm up our muscles. I hope you don't mind beginning work tonight, Madame, I mean, Alice."

"How many people come?" Liberty asked.

"Hundreds."

Surely, out of hundreds of people, some will have seen the signs. "Can I wear a disguise—I mean, a costume?"

"Madame Torso said she'd bring her own."

"I have an extra wig," Carl offered. "It's rainbow colored."

"I'll try it."

Circus tricks

The next four hours were Liberty's most enjoyable ever. Jordan rode her around on the unicycle. Vrushenka let her swing on the trapeze.

Maybe I don't need to go to the Sullivan School, she thought. *Here is someplace I can belong.* The one thing she didn't think about was what it might feel like to perform in front of an audience.

When evening came, and Modesto introduced her (as the Amazing Alice) and the spotlight poured onto her, Liberty's heart practically stopped. Her mouth became cotton and her whole body shook.

Modesto had instructed her to run to the center of the stage and bow to each part of the audience. Instead, she dashed straight to the cage, opened it, and slipped inside.

"The Amazing Alice is eager to see Godwin, the world's most dangerous lion," Modesto shouted to the crowd. "She doesn't even use a whip!"

World's most dangerous? Liberty thought. *He should've told me that before.*

The audience applauded.

"Hello, Godwin," Liberty said nervously.

"Did you bring more food?" He'd had a few hot dogs, but his appetite had been whetted rather than satisfied.

"Stories. Remember."

"Oh, yeah."

"While I tell you a story, we entertain the audience, right?"

"I suppose." Godwin yawned.

"What do we do?" The audience was shifting with impatience.

"I roar. You put your head in my mouth."

Liberty wasn't sure that was a great plan.

"Now the Amazing Alice will put her head inside Godwin the Terrible's mouth. Will he snap it off?" Modesto shouted.

Godwin roared and opened his mouth.

With the clown wig, Liberty's head didn't really fit. Still, the crowd cheered.

"I'm waiting for my story," Godwin said.

"What?" Liberty couldn't quite make out his words. *Is it the noise from the crowd?* she wondered. The one word she heard was "story." So she began. "Once upon a time, there was a lion called Godwin. One morning, he woke up to find that something very unusual had happened."

Godwin paced back and forth. He nudged her arm. The audience applauded. "I can't hear you very well."

"Godwin had sprouted wings. There, coming out of his back like two extra shoulders, were triangles covered in gold and silver feathers." Liberty waved her hands in the air. The crowd clapped again.

Godwin roared his hot-ketchup-and-hot-dog breath into her face. "Louder. I can barely make out the words."

Liberty froze. She realized that it had been at least a day since she had heard the sound of nature. Was the comprehension cream wearing off? "Imagine his surprise," Liberty shouted inside to Godwin.

Godwin pawed at the ground and roared.

"Godwin!" She could no longer comprehend him. Nor could he understand *her*. She began to yell the story out loud. "The first thing Godwin wanted to do was to try out these new wings. So he climbed the tallest mountain—"

Godwin roared again. *If she can't tell me a story,* he thought, *I'll have her for dessert.* Swinging one massive paw, Godwin knocked Liberty to the other side of the cage. Only her wig was left behind, like a disembodied head.

The crowd gasped. Confused, Godwin picked up the wig and shook it in his mouth.

Dizzily, Liberty scrambled to her feet.

"Move the spotlight! Move the spotlight!" she heard Modesto shout.

But Jordan had abandoned the spotlight and was rushing to the concession stand for hot dogs.

Luckily, cats like to play with their prey before eating it. Dropping the wig, Godwin moved slowly toward Liberty. He swatted her again with his paw. She heard her dress rip, but she remained standing.

Godwin crouched low, ready to pounce.

Liberty looked behind her to see if there was an exit. There wasn't.

But there was one thing there: the mirror. Quickly, she lifted it and held it up to Godwin's face.

Godwin straightened up and gazed into the mirror. So dazzled was Godwin by his gorgeous mane, his round, inquisitive eyes, his fabulous whiskers, that he froze on the spot.

The crowd cheered. Cameras flashed around her.

Liberty knew that Godwin's vanity couldn't last forever. Holding the mirror in front of her, she began slowly edging around the cage toward the door on the other side. Hypnotically gazing at himself, Godwin followed.

Jordan arrived with a tray of hot dogs and began pelting the lion with the food.

It broke the spell. Godwin began eating the hot dogs. Liberty dropped the mirror and made a dash for the door, which Jordan had opened. She slid out just as Godwin finished the last hot dog.

"Bow!" Modesto called to her. "Bow!"

Liberty bowed.

The crowd went wild with applause.

A word about worms

There are lots of good things about worms. Worms add nitrogen and good bacteria to the soil, enabling plants and trees to grow. Trees give us oxygen.

Worms do not pollute, start wars, gossip, or tell bad jokes. Worms work together as a community, rather than just looking out for themselves.

One of the first people to seriously study worms was the famed naturalist Charles Darwin. Darwin studied worms for over thirty years. The last book he wrote was about them.

Darwin learned, from experiments, that while worms are blind, deaf, and spineless, they have their own kind of intelligence. They can sense light and danger.

Worms also like moisture. In order for Worm Man to get his worms to burrow to the depth that he wanted, he had to design an underground irrigation system to attract them with moisture.

Mal wasn't the only inventor around.

The more Edgar dug his tunnel, the more he felt the need to rescue Sally. He tried *not* to think about the prospect that he hadn't seen Sally because she had met some sad fate. Certainly, as many times as he had knocked on the door since Mal left, no one had answered.

So he had sped up the construction of his tunnel. He would find out once and for all if she was there. His plan was to go in through the basement while Mal was out. "Must. Save. Sally," he told himself when the digging tired him. "Must save her." Even if she didn't need it.

The Arrival of Madame Torso

Liberty awakened to the sound of voices just outside the trailer.

"What a performance," Modesto was saying.

"I can't wait to see the papers," Carl said.

"We not put girl in danger again," Vrushenka said. "I train her for trapeze."

"Nonsense," Modesto said. "We'll just have to buy a new mirror each night. There must be somewhere we can get them wholesale."

Liberty sat up in bed. Her ribs were bruised. Her head ached. No way was she going back into that cage. Sadly, she would have to leave.

She was about to go out and tell them when she heard terrifying sounds, as if guns fired, crowds screamed, and herds of zebras stampeded all at once. *Could it be Mal?* She crawled under the bed and hid.

"Madame," she heard Modesto shout, "you have just widened the entrance to the tent by about fifty feet."

A trumpet sounded. It was the tune used on *Queen for Once.*

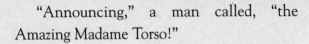

"Announcing," a man called, "the Amazing Madame Torso!"

Liberty came out from under the bed, crept to the door, and peered out. There were no zebras, just two horses with a carriage attached. The driver wore a cowboy hat and bandana. He was helping a lady down the steps of the carriage. Her hair was bright orange and piled high upon her head. Her face was as lined as the world's oldest piece of leather. She cracked a whip in the air.

Vrushenka, Carl, and Modesto stood staring. Jordan was nowhere in sight.

"The future has arrived," Madame Torso said in a loud but shaky voice. "And it is not very interesting. Everything is about machines.

There was a time when we fought *not* to be machines. Now, here we are. The machine age. Technology. The circus, though, is the antidote, the cure."

Shyly, Liberty tiptoed outside and stood next to Vrushenka, who pulled her close.

"And now," Madame Torso said, "to the details. I will need my own trailer. You only have one, I see. I will take it. Everyone else can sleep in a tent. I work two hours a day. The rest of the time, I get my beauty rest."

"I am not sleeping in tent!" Vrushenka remonstrated.

"Well," Modesto said, much more gently, "my dear Madame Torso. As impressive as your credentials are, we already have a lion tamer, as it turns out."

But they don't, Liberty thought. If she got into the cage again without the comprehension cream, Godwin would eat her for sure.

"I, the Amazing Madame Torso, have a contract." She snapped her fingers. Her driver rushed into the coach and brought back a roll of toilet paper, which he tossed to the ground. As it unrolled, Liberty saw that there was writing on the whole thing. At the end was a large and elaborate signature: *Modesto Impregno.*

"Is that not you?" Madame Torso looked at Modesto. "Did you not sign this, little green man?"

Modesto looked at his feet. "Well, yes."

"You signed such a thing?" Carl said. "Did you even read it?"

"It's toilet paper," Modesto defended himself. "It was all rolled up."

"Well, I'll flush it." Vrushenka grabbed the loose paper and began to ball it up.

"I have copies." Madame Torso tapped her foot. "So . . . where is this . . . imposter who tried to steal my job?"

Modesto swept his hand toward Liberty, who blushed from head to toe.

"This . . . child? She is no lion tamer. Where did you study, I want to know?" Madame Torso poked a craggy finger at Liberty.

"I'm homeschooled," Liberty answered meekly.

"You have lions at home?"

Liberty didn't get to reply. Zipping in on his unicycle, Jordan arrived, balancing a stack of newspapers on his head. He jumped off and held up the first paper. The front-page photo was of Liberty, holding the mirror to Godwin's face. LION HYPNOTIZED BY THE AMAZING ALICE. Her wig had come off. Even without her braids, she looked like herself. What if Mal saw the photo?

Jordan held up another newspaper, one with an even closer shot of her. CIRCUS BRINGS FRESH TAKE TO LION TAMING.

THE AMAZING ALICE DELIGHTS AUDIENCES, another said.

Madame Torso's mouth dropped open in horror.

"You see." Modesto pointed to yet another newspaper photo. "The Amazing Alice is a famous lion tamer."

Fame is something that many people want, but Liberty already knew that it was a lot more trouble than it was worth. "I have to go."

"Now you're talking," Madame Torso said.

"But you our star," Vrushenka said.

Liberty burst into tears. She told them about running away (minus the flying part) and about Mal chasing after her. "He'll see these newspapers and know that I'm here."

"Tragic," Modesto said.

"If you hand me over to him, you'll get ten thousand dollars," Liberty admitted. "That's the reward."

"Really?" Modesto perked up. "We could afford a new trailer with that for our dear Madame Torso."

"Modesto!" Vrushenka whacked him with a newspaper. "We will not turn in friend Alice! We are honorable people. Not greedy. Sometimes honorable people are poor, like us. That how we got so poor. Being too honorable. But it is worth it for self-respect."

"Yes, being poor is so terribly honorable," Carl said.

Jordan gestured a question: *Where will you go?*

"Yes," Carl said. "Do tell us where you'll go."

"Boarding school."

"But which one?" Carl asked. "Some are not that great."

Liberty hesitated. But they were her friends. "The Sullivan School."

"*I* went to the Sullivan School. It is a most remarkable place of higher education, as you can see." Madame Torso gestured to herself.

Jordan began weeping silently.

"Thank you for saving my life with hot dogs." Liberty hugged him. She turned to Modesto. "Why isn't Jordan in the show? He can juggle and ride the unicycle, and he has a wonderful face and gestures. He would make such a terrific clown."

Jordan's face went red, but he nodded frantically as if he agreed.

"Maybe that's why he came to you in the first place."

"Jordan cooks and cleans," Carl snapped. "We need him for that."

Modesto put a hand to his chin. "I never considered it before. And he's never asked. But you're right. Jordan *would* make a wonderful clown."

"Boy does seem talented," Madame Torso said. She was in a much better mood now that her job was reinstated.

"But *I* am the clown." Carl stomped his foot.

"Two clowns would be even funnier," Liberty said.

Jordan bowed at everyone. Carl scowled.

"But not two lion tamers," Madame Torso said.

"Yes. Can you tell me how to get to the school?"

"Certainly. It is just past Fairhaven, right along the river. On the other side of Fairhaven are the Sullivan Woods. Walk through the woods; otherwise you have to

drive all the way around. Tell them I sent you. I am famous there."

"Have a potato for the journey." Vrushenka brought
one from the bin.

Suddenly, Jordan pointed. The walls of the tent were
being pushed violently. "Blasted thing," came Mal's ma-
licious voice. "Where is the entrance?"

"It's him!" Liberty panicked.

"Not to worry." Madame Torso pulled out a pistol. "I
will shoot him dead."

It was a tempting idea. "I'll just go. I don't want you
to get in trouble." Liberty ran to the back of the tent and
slipped out the small gap, the same way she'd entered.

A moment later, Jordan appeared with his unicycle.
"Jordan, you don't have to take me."

In answer, Jordan scooped her up and leapt onto
the unicycle.

Behind them, they heard Mal. "Where is she? She's
my private property! I own her. I'm going to teach her
a lesson!"

Journey

As they cycled toward the river, a light rain fell. It reminded Liberty of tears. For a single day, she had belonged somewhere, and what a wonderful feeling that had been. Now it was over.

As if Jordan sensed her feelings, he reached back and squeezed her arm.

"Do you remember Madame Torso's directions?" Liberty asked.

Jordan nodded.

"You're sure?" The last time he'd brought her not to the school, but to the circus. "Why *did* you bring me to the circus before?"

In answer, Jordan made the unicycle spin. A few passersby applauded. He hopped the cycle off a curb, then headed straight down a steep hill.

Liberty clutched him tightly. "You played a part in my destiny. And maybe *I* played a part in yours."

That was how things worked, she was beginning to realize. Destiny wasn't something you accomplished by yourself.

As if in agreement, the sun came out. The sky cleared; the river appeared at the bottom of the hill.

"You don't have to take me the *whole* way," Liberty told Jordan. "You have things to do at the circus. Madame Torso is bound to be interesting."

He shook his head, emphatically. Liberty could tell he wasn't happy about Madame Torso. Madame Torso reminded her of a witch in a fairy tale, who might decide to turn someone into a toad, then change her mind and turn them back. She wasn't all bad, but not all good either. To think she'd gone to the Sullivan School.

At the river, Jordan came to a stop. He pointed one way, then the other.

"Let me check. I want to make sure I get this right." Liberty took out the map and her pen. This time, she found the streets on the map. She drew a line to guide her. "Yes! We're on our way."

Splat! The white "paint" landed right next to the wheel. Liberty looked up. "Birdbrain!" Her heart lifted.

Jordan put his hands on his hips.

"Not you, Jordan. It's my friend. He helped me when I was kidnapped."

Liberty held out her arm. Birdbrain landed.

"You crossed the water. Did you see the newspaper?" Birdbrain cooed.

"How sad. I can't understand you anymore, although I'll bet you understand me. We're still looking for the Sullivan School. This is my friend Jordan. Do you want to come along?"

Birdbrain hopped onto her shoulder and hung on as they zipped off on the unicycle.

As they rode along, they got plenty of attention. Some people recognized Liberty as the circus girl. Luckily, because her braids were gone, few recognized her from the signs.

Occasionally, when a child called out to her, Liberty waved. "Come to the circus tonight. See Jordan, the amazing clown."

She might as well advertise.

Into the woods

It would be a wonderful thing if glee and excitement were lasting emotions. But, like balloons, spaceships, and airplanes, what goes up must come down.

The trio rode along in high spirits for another hour or so, but then Liberty began to notice how very uncomfortable the seat was, how hungry she was, and how sharp Birdbrain's claws were, clutching the shoulder of her torn dress.

The city had given way to a town, then to miles of highway, all looking the same. Would she ever find Fairhaven?

The trio stopped for a moment, searched for signs of Mal, then shared the raw potato. It felt like a stone in Liberty's stomach.

They had just begun traveling again when Liberty noticed something, a pointed spire in the sky, like the one on No Name's church. "I think that's a church," she said. "Let's keep going."

Soon the church came into clear view. Next to it was a school. Then a post office appeared and a library: FAIRHAVEN FREE LIBRARY. Soon they were in a very nice downtown complete with an ice cream shop, a movie theater, and a drugstore.

"This is it!" Liberty tapped Jordan. "Finally."

Fairhaven was one of those towns that in the old days would've been known as a one-horse town. (Madame Torso was old enough to have ridden a horse into such a town.) It consisted of a single main street, a four-way stoplight, and a couple of cozy neighborhoods with clapboard houses.

"Now we have to find the Sullivan Woods."

Liberty tried to let excitement keep her going, even as her mood was sinking; she would soon say goodbye to Jordan. Sure enough, the highway reappeared, and then they saw the sign: SULLIVAN WOODS. SANCTUARY FOR BIRD AND GAME. "Sanctuary for birds! You'll like this, Birdbrain."

Jordan stopped the unicycle and they hopped off.

"Madame Torso said it was on the other side of these woods," Liberty told him. "I'm afraid the unicycle won't help us."

Jordan tapped his chest and pointed.

Liberty hugged him. "You have to go back now, Jordan. Remember, you're performing tonight. I'll bet you're the star of the show."

He made cheering gestures.

"Thank you for taking me."

He frowned.

"Birdbrain will keep me company. Don't worry. I'll be

fine. And you can visit me at the Sullivan School, but just in case, I'll give you my other address. If my father manages to catch me, I'll be at Thirty-three Gooch Street. It's outside the city. Can you remember that?"

Birdbrain nodded.

"I mean Jordan, silly." She stroked Birdbrain's back. "Will you remember, Jordan?"

Jordan looked panicked. He shook his head.

"Never mind. I'll find *you*. A circus is easier to find than a girl. Right?" After one last hug, Liberty watched Jordan ride away. He didn't do his usual jumps and spins. Instead, he rode with his head down. Lackluster.

"He doesn't talk," Liberty said sadly, "yet it felt like we communicated perfectly." She blinked back tears. "Like you, Birdbrain. I'm so glad you're here. I guess we should start through the woods, although I'm a bit scared. In stories, strange things always happen in the woods."

They started out, Birdbrain perched on Liberty's shoulder. After a few minutes, she realized that rather than being frightening, the trees, the soft leaves, and the pine needles beneath her feet gave her a peaceful feeling. Although she couldn't hear nature's subtle music without the comprehension cream, she could somehow *feel* it. If she weren't in such a hurry, she would've liked to stop and examine every spiderweb and bird nest, the fascinating pattern of tree bark.

Sal would enjoy such things too, she thought, *if only she'd leave the house!*

All of a sudden, Liberty heard a man's voice. She ducked behind a tree.

"I'm starving," the man said.

"It was your appetite that got us here in the first place." *Oh no!* It was the shrill, nasty voice of Lola.

"What I wouldn't give for a bowl of that oatmeal," Albert whined.

"Oh shut up! You've been going on about oatmeal for two days."

"One day," Albert said.

"Two," Lola argued. "And in case you haven't figured it out, it was the oatmeal that put us up here in the first place!"

Up? Liberty stood, slowly.

"You wanted to bump the poor child off," Albert said.

"I should've. Because of the *poor child* we're going to die of starvation stuck in a tree!"

"Find them," she whispered to Birdbrain. "But don't let them see you."

Birdbrain swooped up.

"Die?" Albert said. "Who said anything about dying?"

Birdbrain soon came back, then darted away. Liberty followed, looking up until she spotted four legs dangling from a high branch in one of the tallest trees. Albert was missing a shoe.

She giggled as she tiptoed away, but the farther she

got, the more her conscience pricked her, like a wasp carrying a pitchfork.

They'd been up there since yesterday, without eating or having shelter. If someone didn't rescue them, they could indeed perish.

What can I do? she thought. "Why should I bother -161 with them?" she asked Birdbrain. "I need to get to school. Still . . ." She stopped and tore a piece of ocean, blank and blue, off her map, and took out her pen. *Two people are trapped in the treetops in the Sullivan Woods near Fairhaven*, she wrote. *Please send help.*

"Birdbrain, I have a job for you. Do you understand?"

Birdbrain's head moved a bit. Liberty hoped that meant yes. "Take this message to town. Give the note to someone."

Birdbrain took the paper but didn't fly.

"I can't leave them up there."

Birdbrain pecked her face gently, a bird kiss.

"We'll find each other again. I'll be at the Sullivan

School, just through the woods. Once I'm a student, I'll find nice table scraps for you and set them out every day. You're a homing pigeon, I think. I've read about them. You'll always be able to find me. Go on now."

Birdbrain lifted off, glancing back. Liberty could tell that he was sad to be leaving her but also happy to be of use, to have a purpose.

Liberty began to run. She wanted to be through the woods when people came to rescue the two.

Passing over the scoundrels, Birdbrain couldn't help but make a bit of mischief and art, which landed on Lola's head. Liberty heard her outraged scream ring through the woods. It is a well-known fact that pigeons do not laugh. But Birdbrain did coo, his own version of a chuckle.

A thorny situation

Liberty traveled a long time. The bickering voices of Albert and Lola faded. She hoped never to hear them again.

She was sorry that Birdbrain was gone, although there hadn't been much of a choice. She couldn't just leave them up there, especially not Albert. Now, if it had been just Lola . . .

A sharp pain stung her neck. She slapped at a mosquito. From summers on Gooch Street she knew they were a bad sign, because they arrived in the early evening.

The sky *did* seem darker. Still no Sullivan School. What if she was going in the wrong direction? She looked at her map, but it was of no help in the woods.

Emotions are complicated things. As Liberty walked she felt several all at once: sadness, that her friends were gone; fear, that she was stuck in the woods forever; and excitement, that she was finally on her way.

"Ouch!" Her foot came up against a small rosebush in full bloom. "Oh!"

The roses *rose*. A small face surrounded by thorns and petals greeted her. It was the snake from Mal's lab. Pinned to him like layers of colored gossamer were several skins he had shed, still held to his body by the thorny branches.

"What a miracle to find you here!" Liberty cried out. "The blossoms look beautiful, but you must be so uncomfortable. Should I try to remove the branches?" She lifted the snake and sat down on a large stone. Trying to avoid the thorns, she gently worked a branch free, then rubbed the wound. "I hope this doesn't hurt." She started on another. "I remember a book with a yellow snake in it. It was about a prince who comes to earth. In the end, he

learns a lesson from a fox. 'One sees clearly only with the heart.' It's funny, I remember the words exactly." She told the snake about the book until she worked the last branch free.

Gleeful, the snake snaked (for lack of a better word) off Liberty's lap and twisted through the leaves, its old skins dropping. When he returned, he was a new color, a lovely shade of green.

"I don't suppose you can lead me to the Sullivan School?"

The snake rose up and peered at her, but didn't seem to understand. Birdbrain had, though; she was sure of it. Even without comprehension cream.

The snake swirled in a circle. Then, with a whisk of its tail, it slipped away through the brush.

"Alone again. *Great.*" She began trudging through the woods again. "Which is worse? To be hungry or lonely?" she asked the trees. "To be lonely. Definitely."

The more she walked, the darker it got, and the more the mosquitoes came. If someone were watching Liberty from a distance, she would've resembled a crazed dancer, ducking and slapping at the mosquitoes.

Finally, it all became too much for her. Looking around and seeing no shelter in sight, she pushed leaves, pine

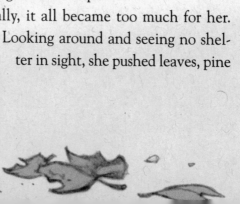

needles, and moss into a giant mound. She then bur-
rowed under so that even her face was covered. Promptly,
she fell into a sleep so deep she didn't notice her new
insect friends *under* the ground, much nicer bedfellows
than mosquitoes.

Worms.

Trespassing

There were several things that woke Liberty from her deep, exhausted sleep. The leaves had become cold and damp, despite the midmorning sun shining down. A fly buzzed in her ear. Her face and neck itched, and as she scratched, she felt the welts of the mosquito bites.

She stood up and brushed off as much of the leaves and dirt as she could.

A few moments later, she heard voices from an area above her, where the bank sloped up toward a plateau. *I think this is it!*

The hill was steeper than it looked. Liberty climbed on her hands and knees so she wouldn't slide, grabbing the earth with her fingers and digging in with her worn-out shoes.

What she saw when she reached the top was stunning: a green lawn stretching as far as she could see and the huge, majestic brick building, like a castle in a fairy tale, that she recognized from the brochure.

She had arrived. Finally. Liberty felt like dashing across the lawn, bursting through the door of the building, and shouting, like a child who'd run from school through a rainstorm, "I'm home!"

Across the lawn, a row of boys and girls marched in a line behind a teacher, a tall man with a walking stick. The boys wore navy pants, white shirts, and gray sweaters. The girls wore gray plaid skirts (gray!), crisp white shirts, and gray sweaters. When Liberty saw them all, so orderly and uniform, she felt like another person lived inside her skin, a much smaller one. And that person shrank deep within herself.

In other words, she felt shy.

Laughing and talking, the students marched past without noticing her. Several times, the teacher turned and held a finger up to his lips to silence them.

Liberty waited until they were past, then she followed, ducking behind the many trees that dotted the campus.

The teacher and children entered a smaller building. It reminded her of the houses she'd seen when she climbed out of the sewer. There were beautiful flowers all around it, and a beech tree that spread like an umbrella over the building, dwarfing it.

Liberty considered following them inside, but then she had another idea. She jumped on one of the tree's low branches and began to climb. From the midsection, she could see in the windows of the second floor, where children were walking quickly down the hall and filing into rooms. She scurried to another limb.

From there she saw inside an entire classroom with

lovely wooden desks in a row. This teacher reminded her of illustrations of Mother Goose. She had gray hair piled on her head and little pinchy glasses.

After the children filled the desks, the teacher began to talk, pointing to various places on a large, colorful map.

The map fascinated Liberty. She longed to hear what the teacher was saying.

Each child had a box of colored pencils on their desk. While the teacher talked, the children colored in their own maps, although a couple of girls were whispering to each other and a boy at the back of the room was shooting wads of paper out of his mouth.

Liberty watched the teacher for a long time, trying to imagine what she was saying. How she longed to be inside, listening and coloring in her own map.

Suddenly, a bell rang. Children began pouring out of the building, carrying lunch trays. Food! They sat on the ground or on benches that dotted the lawn.

What are they eating? Liberty wondered. She was so hungry. She scurried along the tree branches like a squirrel, then climbed lower so she could see.

Beneath her, a group of girls sat at a picnic table. On their trays were noodles, sandwiches, cups of soup, strawberries, carrots, potato chips, and cookies.

Liberty's mouth watered.

"Tell us more, Riley," a blond girl was saying.

"I'm going to have my party beside the swimming

pool," Riley said. "There'll be dancing. It's going to be catered with drinks that have umbrellas in them and canapés."

"Ohhhh!" two other girls exclaimed in unison.

"What if it rains?" a dark-haired girl said. The words actually came out kind of mushy, as she had new braces.

"It never rains in July, Brace Face," Riley said.

"Are you going to invite all of us?" the blond asked.

Invite me, Liberty thought, crawling onto a lower branch to hear more and to smell the wonderful food.

Let's shift the point of view for just a moment to the six girls in starched white shirts and gray plaid skirts (I am what is known as an omniscient narrator, so I am allowed to do so). They were discussing the menu for a summer party, when out of nowhere, a girl dropped out of a tree, *smack,* on top of their lunches. The girl was filthy, with welts on her face and neck, a torn dress, and a bad haircut.

What did they think?

Actually, some were curious. The one with the braces was terribly worried that the girl was hurt.

Riley, who was bragging about her party, however, was horrified to have such a wretched creature upstage her. "Oh my God! Look at the freak the cat dragged in." She pointed.

Somehow cats are involved in everything. Liberty scrambled off the table.

"And look what it did to our lunches!" someone else said.

Picking up the cue, two others joined in. "It's a freak from the sky!"

Brace Face opened her mouth to speak. She was going to say, *Give the kid a break and let's find out if she's hurt*, but unfortunately she had just taken a bite of peanut butter sandwich and her braces were stuck together.

"You're trespassing, street person!" Riley shouted.

Liberty tried to wipe the food from her dress. "But I'm supposed to live here," she explained in a small voice.

"You've got to be joking," Riley said.

"Trespasser! Trespasser!" two girls chanted.

A girl with glasses appeared from the other side of the tree. "How can I study with you geese squawking?" -173

"Some street person snuck into the school!" Riley said.

"Lost, are you?" the girl asked.

"She thinks she's supposed to live here!" Riley made a gagging gesture.

"Ignore them," the girl said. "They're a bunch of scoundrels."

Even here, at the Sullivan School, there were scoundrels.

"You're not going to be invited to my party, Joelly!" Riley taunted.

"*Whatever.*" Joelly took Liberty's arm. "I'd better take you to admissions. You have to be admitted before you can live here."

As Joelly wandered with Liberty across the lovely grounds, pointing out the swimming complex, the ice-skating rink, and the huge glass library, Liberty forgot about the mean girls and became happy again. She could feel it inside, like a cup of hot chocolate warming her on a snowy day: She *was* going to live at the Sullivan School.

Vice

Joelly led Liberty to the administration building. "Let's brush some of the food and leaves off of you before we go in. I'll bet you have a good story to tell me about this one day."

"I do!" Liberty said.

"Mrs. Vice handles admissions. She's a cranky old bird, so I'll stand by and make sure everything goes okay."

Liberty followed Joelly into the grand building and up a huge wooden staircase.

Mrs. Vice, sadly, was one who judges others on appearances, although her own was not so hot. She had a gray shriveled face and a mouth that puckered like she'd swallowed a lemon.

She took one look at Liberty and raised a newspaper in front of her face. "We don't need any new employees." Ignoring people was her puny way of feeling powerful, when her job was to help them.

"Excuse me, Mrs. Vice," Joelly said.

Mrs. Vice turned to the weddings page. She liked to look at the smiling brides and imagine how miserable they would soon be.

But Joelly wasn't one to be ignored. She rapped on Mrs. Vice's desk like it was a door. "A prospective student is here."

"All I see is a street urchin who isn't clean enough to work in the kitchen."

"I would like to begin school at once," Liberty said.

"At once? School will be out in five weeks, and the students will return home. We are certainly not accepting applications for *this* term!"

Liberty's heart sank. *Returning home?* She had assumed that once you went to boarding school, you stayed forever.

"Well, give her an application for next year, then," Joelly demanded.

"The deadline has passed. The selection process is closed." Mrs. Vice held the newspaper up in front of her face again.

"Wait here. I'll get the head teacher," Joelly told Liberty, and dashed off.

"Madame Torso sent me," Liberty offered.

"Madame who?"

"She went here, about . . . ninety years ago."

"Some dead person is of no interest to me." Mrs. Vice kept the newspaper firmly in front of her face.

Liberty looked at the paper more closely. There was her face with the words MISSING CHILD underneath it.

Joelly reappeared, tugging a lady who looked young enough to be a student. "Mrs. Vice? What is going on?"

To Liberty's relief, Mrs. Vice put the newspaper down.

"This *child*"—Mrs. Vice spit the words out like a nasty bit of food—"wants to attend the Sullivan School."

"Well, give her an application, then."

"The deadline has passed." Mrs. Vice winked.

"It has not!" the teacher said.

"*Look* at her."

Liberty winced as the teacher looked her up and down, afraid she might agree with Mrs. Vice, but the teacher smiled and then turned back to the old secretary. "You seem to have forgotten the story of Carol Sullivan, who started the school that employs you."

"Times have changed since then!"

"The mission of this school has never changed. The Sullivan School *does not* discriminate. You will please give her an application." The teacher turned to Liberty and held out her hand. "What is your name?"

"Liberty Aimes."

"I am Ms. Klaus." The teacher shook her hand. "Like Santa Claus, only with a *K*. Thank you for coming to get me, Joelly. You'd better return to lunch. I don't want any growling stomachs in Botany this afternoon."

"Good luck!" Joelly gave Liberty a thumbs-up. Liberty watched her slide down the banister. Perhaps she would do that some day.

Ms. Klaus snapped the application out of Mrs. Vice's hand and gave it to Liberty. "Your parents need to fill this out and sign it. The deadline is in two weeks, so please have them return it quickly."

"My parents?"

"Yes, we must have a parent's signature."

"I'll bet she doesn't have any." Mrs. Vice snickered. "She belongs in an orphanage."

"Mrs. Vice, hold your tongue."

Scoundrel, Liberty felt like adding, but she wisely held *her* tongue.

"Of course she has parents," Ms. Klaus said, but she wasn't too sure. The child in front of her looked like she'd been living on the streets. "Don't you?"

Liberty nodded.

"Good."

"She needs her school transcripts, too," Mrs. Vice added.

"School transcripts?" Liberty asked.

"The record of your previous years at school," Ms. Klaus explained.

"I'm homeschooled."

"In that case, there are tests to take. Don't worry. We have several children admitted who were homeschooled. What grade will you be entering?"

"I don't know."

"Well, how old are you?"

Liberty thought hard. Her birthday was in the spring, not that her parents ever celebrated it. "Ten. Or maybe eleven. What date is it?"

"April twentieth."

"I guess I'm still ten."

"Ridiculous," Mrs. Vice said.

"Can you read?" Ms. Klaus asked.

"Oh yes, I've read lots of books."

"What's the last book you read?"

"*Alice in Wonderland.*"

"Splendid. Can you do math?"

"Yes. And I can lay bricks, too."

"Hah!" Mrs. Vice guffawed. "There's also a five-thousand-dollar deposit due with the application."

A lump formed in Liberty's throat. There was no chance of her ever coming up with five thousand dollars, let alone her parents' signatures. "F-five thousand dollars?"

"Come, let's take a walk." Ms. Klaus took Liberty's arm and led her outside. "Then we can look over the application together. I'll bet you haven't even had lunch."

"No. Not breakfast, either."

Ms. Klaus shook her head, which meant *Something is awry, and I'm going to get to the bottom of it.*

They strolled down a sloping path that gave a view of the school grounds and took them past beautiful gardens.

"You'll have to forgive Mrs. Vice for being so rude. Five out of her six marriages made her bitter."

"What about the sixth?" Liberty asked.

"The wedding was a week ago. So far, so good."

"Who was Carol Sullivan?" Liberty asked.

"A girl who grew up in an orphanage. She had no formal education, but she was very clever. At the orphanage, her job was to fix things. When she grew up, she invented objects to help make women's lives easier."

"What did she invent?"

"The mechanism that went inside the first washing machine. A motorized sewing machine. Lots of other things. Once she became wealthy, she started the Sullivan School. It was originally an orphanage, but unlike the one where she grew up, it gave orphans an education equal to that of the best schools. It went on that way for about fifty years, but eventually the endowment wasn't enough to keep up with costs, and orphans were placed with families instead of in institutions. This then became a private school." They came to a small cottage. "This is where I live," Ms. Klaus said. "We'll have lunch and then I can help you with the application."

"Lunch," Liberty said. The mere thought of eating made her knees go weak. Everything went dark.

Lunch

Liberty awoke on a couch in a sunny room. Ms. Klaus was sitting on the chair across from her. "You fainted. I was about to call a doctor."

"I'm fine. Just hungry."

"Well, I've got your lunch all ready. Stay there. I'll serve you on a tray."

I suppose you would like it if Liberty were served an elaborate feast, like pineapple spears, cheese fondue, chocolate crepes, and broiled lobster. The truth is, if you haven't eaten for a while, it's best to start out with something simple.

Ms. Klaus brought a tray with a bowl of noodle soup, a thick grilled cheese sandwich, and a tall glass of milk.

"Thank you," Liberty said.

"When *was* the last time you ate?"

Liberty tried to remember. "Yesterday I had part of a raw potato."

Ms. Klaus pulled her chair closer. "So, tell me . . . *are* you an orphan?"

"No, I have parents," Liberty said, regretfully.

"Did you run away from home?"

Liberty chewed a big bite of sandwich. "I flew."

"You were in a hurry?"

"I went pretty fast."

"How long have you been away?"

"A few days."

"Are there problems at home, then?"

"I don't want to be homeschooled."

"Aha. I see." Ms. Klaus looked
at her watch. "I'm afraid I have
an afternoon class. Promise me
you'll stay right here until I get
back."

"I promise." Liberty wanted to stay forever.

"Why don't you take a bath. There're plenty of towels. You can put your dress into the washing machine, or maybe . . . maybe you should just throw it out. In the closet, you will find several school uniforms. They used to be mine when I was a student here. One of them should fit you."

"I get to wear a school uniform?"

"I think that dress has seen better days."

Liberty looked down, blushing. "I guess so."

"I'll be back as soon as I can."

After Ms. Klaus left, Liberty carried her dishes to the sink and washed up.

She filled the bath with hot water and poured in soap to make bubbles. The last time she had done so was for Mal. Could that have only been days ago?

She went to the closet. On one side were six or seven uniforms. Liberty chose one that looked just her size and

hung it on a hook in the bathroom. *Gray.* Oh well. She'd wait until she was a grown-up to wear colors.

It was delightful to throw her filthy dress away, like the snake discarding its skin. She looked at the school uniform that she would soon wear, as if she was already fulfilling her destiny.

Slipping into the warm water, she closed her eyes and floated, luxuriating in being clean and safe at last. And as she floated, a nursery rhyme came into her head. It was from the first book she'd read. *Jack Sprat could eat no fat, his wife could eat no lean. And so betwixt the two of them, they licked the platter clean.*

Like Jack Sprat, Mal never ate, not even the butter-goo pudding he made for Sal. But Sal licked all the platters clean.

Liberty opened her eyes. Why did he make that pudding for Sal when he never lifted a finger for her otherwise? And why wasn't *she* allowed to eat it? Why was he always pushing food at Sal? He was too cheap to heat the house, but he didn't mind buying food. Why was he always encouraging Sal to eat more and more?

The answer popped into her mind. *To keep her trapped.*

The sad truth

Liberty was still in the bath when Ms. Klaus returned. The hot water had soothed her tired and aching body, which had taken quite a beating over the past few days.

"I'll be right out," Liberty called.

"There's an extra toothbrush in the cabinet, and a hairbrush in the drawer should you need it."

"Thank you."

"I'll make some tea."

Liberty dressed quickly, but she couldn't help lingering at the mirror, staring at herself in the Sullivan School uniform (and reminding herself to fix her haircut soon).

"Don't you look perfect!" Ms. Klaus said. "Come to the table. I've got some cupcakes."

"Thank you." Liberty sat down happily.

"We can fill out the application together . . ." Ms. Klaus looked down at the table, then back up. "Then I'll take you home."

"But . . . I don't want to go home."

"It's against the law for me to harbor a runaway."

"I'm going to go to the school. Aren't I?" Liberty fought back the tears that sprang to her eyes.

"I hope so, and I will help you all I can. But the school won't admit you without your parents' permission."

Here it was. Defeat. She was not free to do as she wanted. Her parents, as Mal had so often said, owned her.

"How about this?" Ms. Klaus offered. "I'll talk to your parents and try to convince them that school would be the best thing for you."

"They'll say no."

"You have a right to go to school. It's the law. If things are *very* bad at home, sometimes the state can intervene."

That sounded a bit more hopeful. "You mean the state can *make* my parents send me to school here?"

"Or somewhere."

"Oh."

"There are even scholarships, if they don't have the money."

"I guess that's all right." There was no other choice, it seemed. The idea of facing Mal made Liberty so sick, she couldn't eat another bite, even though the cupcake was covered with sprinkles. Slowly, they filled out the application.

"Excellent!" Ms. Klaus picked up the form. "I'll just get the car from the garage and pull it round. It's quite a steep hill, so maybe you'd better just rest here and finish your snack. It'll be ten minutes."

"All right," Liberty said sadly.

"I won't leave your parents' house until the forms are signed. I promise!" The front door closed.

Liberty cleared the table and cleaned up.

What would happen when she got home? Would Mal offer Ms. Klaus the ten thousand dollar reward and tell her to go away? Would he lock them both up and experiment upon them? How could Ms. Klaus convince them to send her to school?

I should run away now, Liberty thought, *while she's getting the car.*

She dashed to the door. But what about Ms. Klaus? Here was someone she liked, who wanted to help her, whose clothes she was wearing.

Besides, the Sullivan School was her destiny. She was sure of it. Not even her parents could mess up her destiny. Or could they?

She went outside and watched the road for the car. Everything in Ms. Klaus's garden was blossoming: daffodils and forsythia, a giant dogwood tree. Ms. Klaus herself seemed like a blossom opening up to Liberty and offering help.

A yellow car chugged down the road, came closer. *Ms. Klaus drives a taxicab?* Liberty wondered.

But as the taxi pulled up, Liberty saw that the driver was not Ms. Klaus, but a man with a beard and a turban.

The back door opened, and out hopped a skunk, who immediately sprayed her.

The scent was not the usual dirty-socks smell. This

spray smelled like roses and made Liberty feel like Dorothy in the field of poppies in Oz: so relaxed that she couldn't move a muscle.

Mal popped up in the backseat, jumped out, and dragged her into the cab. "Lesson time!" he said.

Poetry in motion

"What are you doing?" The cabdriver watched them in his mirror.

"My daughter's not feeling well," Mal told him. "Speed up so I can get her home."

Liberty *wasn't* feeling well. She felt like a puddle of water on the pavement.

"Are you sure she's your daughter?" Liberty saw the cabby's worried face in the mirror. With the scrap of energy left in her body, she shook her head. *No! I'm not his daughter.*

"I'd mind my business if I were you, Abdullah Sheik Whateveryourname is," Mal spat. "Parents have rights."

"First, you get in my cab with a skunk," the cabby complained. "Next, you're grabbing people off the street."

Liberty looked out the window. At least her eyes could move. She watched the one lane grow to two, then to a four-lane highway filled with cars. She pondered a sad question. Did Ms. Klaus call Mal and turn her in for the ten thousand dollars?

She thought she had figured out whom to trust, *how* to trust, by going deep inside herself and listening. Could she have been wrong about Ms. Klaus?

As soon as the cabby had his eyes back on the road, Mal leaned toward her. "Where is your dress? That dress cost me ten dollars. You can answer. Only your large muscles are affected."

"How did you find me?" Her voice came out weak.

"Your clown friend told me. He was quite happy to trade that information for a big hamburger and, of course, the ten thousand I assured him I would bring. Fat chance."

"But he doesn't talk!"

"He talked to *me*, gave me an earful about how you ruined his stardom at the circus by having them bring in some mime to upstage him. It's what you do. Ruin things!"

Liberty smiled with relief. So it was Carl, not Jordan or Ms. Klaus. She could tell a friend from a scoundrel, after all.

"I asked you about your dress. Did you trade it for that stupid uniform?"

"You always said you wanted me in boarding school."

"That was just a threat, to make you behave. What kind of moron actually wants to go to boarding school?"

This kind of moron, Liberty almost said, but she wouldn't give Mal the satisfaction.

"More likely I'll send you to a refugee camp or enlist you in the army, Libby-good-for-nothing."

"My name is Liberty!"

Mal glared at her. "You have caused me no end of

trouble and cost me thousands in lost business chasing you around this state. So don't tell me what to call you! And where is my lifting soda, I'd like to know. Did you use it all up?"

Outside the window, the city loomed. Liberty could have wept remembering her old friends there: No Name and Birdbrain, Vrushenka and Jordan. But she didn't want to cry in front of Mal. Didn't want to give him the satisfaction of having the least bit of power over her. "None of your business."

"You'll tell me all right, as soon as we get home." Mal nodded toward the skunk. Liberty could tell he was speaking to it, the way she once could.

The strength was returning to her muscles. She could move her head again. When the cab slowed, she could leap out.

As if it read her thoughts, the skunk jumped up on Mal's lap. "Any false moves and Flowers will spray you again," Mal whispered.

"False moves" was something he'd once heard in a movie.

The cabby's worried face appeared in his mirror. "What is that skunk doing?"

"Reciting poetry," Mal sniped. "So shut up and let me listen."

Nature's garbage disposals

Something happens when you are caring for an animal, or an insect, for that matter. You begin to understand each other. Dogs know when their owner is sad or about to go for a walk. Bees are so attuned to their beekeepers that they won't sting when the keeper puts her hand in the hive to draw out honey.

So it was with Edgar Kind's earthworms. It was as if Edgar had comprehension cream of a different variety, organic, you could say. The worms intuited his need to hurry and were working double shifts on the tunnel.

As Mal snatched Liberty from her liberty, Edgar and his troop of worms had reached the underground wall of the basement. It was now up to him to get through the wall. Using a pickax, Edgar began to strike at the cement. But as the cement fell away, he met up with an even harder wall. "Must. Save. Sally," he chanted, to keep his energy up.

What he didn't know was that the inner walls were almost impossible to penetrate, except in the small areas where Mal had hidden things. Like the third pig in "The Three Little Pigs," Mal had fortified the basement with bricks. Liberty was not the only one who'd read fairy tales.

Edgar beat and beat on that wall, moving from one area to another. *I'll have to get dynamite*, he thought. His pickax hit something soft. He began to work more carefully.

As the hole widened, he shined his flashlight and saw that what he'd hit was a book. Could this be one of Sally's childhood diaries?

The book was wrapped in plastic and deeply embedded in the wall. He couldn't yet pull it out, but he could see writing emerging through the debris.

In large black letters, it said: *Secret Recipes and Inventions*, by Mal Aimes.

The secrets of Mal? It was like discovering an answer without knowing what the question was.

Above him, on the street, Edgar heard a car arrive, doors slam, then Mal's harsh voice. Quickly, he crawled back through his tunnel. The book would have to wait.

Home again, home again, jiggety-jog

As the cab pulled up at 33 Gooch, Liberty took what she supposed was her last look at her neighbors' houses, noticing the terrible contrast their own house made. It was like setting a black-and-white picture down among colored ones.

If you've ever gone on a long vacation or to summer camp, you'll know that returning home can be strange. Once you've adjusted to France or Hawaii or a tent in the Adirondacks, your own house can suddenly feel foreign and strange.

That was how it was with Liberty. After her time in the world with all of its sights, the house seemed drabber and more oppressive than ever, like the world's worst joke.

The skunk ran circles around Liberty, threatening her with its raised tail, as Mal dragged her from the car.

"You'll get no tip from me." Mal thrust money into the cabby's hand. "You do not know your place."

"I've got a tip for you!" the cabby shouted.

But Mal did not wait to hear what it was. With surprising strength, he picked up Liberty and carried her into the house.

The room, too, was much smaller than Liberty remembered. Even her mother, dozing in her favorite chair with the chicken on her lap, seemed shrunken in size.

"What are you doing with my chicken?" Mal yelled.

Sal was startled awake.

"Libby!" Sal set the chicken on the floor and rushed to Liberty. "You're back! Thank goodness! I missed you so much. Your hair! It's short."

Liberty's eyes filled. "You've gotten thinner, Mother."

"I was so worried about you that I lost my appetite. But now I'll get back to eating straightaway. I'll have some clams and pancakes."

"Yes, Mother."

"Wait just a stinking minute," Mal said. "Libby is coming to the basement with me to get her punishment."

"You leave her alone, Mal!" Sal jumped in front of Liberty, and gave Mal a shove that sent him sprawling into the kitchen. "From now on you are not the boss around here!"

"Flowers!" Mal shouted. The skunk rushed over, lifted up her tail, and sprayed Sal. Liberty knew just how Sal felt as she melted to the floor like a puddle of water.

"You'll come with me or be sprayed again, Libby." Mal dragged Liberty down the stairs. She could feel the bones of his hand bruise her skin. The skunk stood in front of Sal, its tail lifted and ready. Clearly, Mal had communicated something to it about guarding her.

"What are you going to do to me?" Liberty asked.

As they entered the basement, she saw all too quickly what would be done with her, for Mal had constructed a large cage. It was about her height and long enough to contain a mattress and chair.

"I just have to put the door on your new home! You've kept me so busy running around the city that I didn't have time to finish. This is where you'll live when you're not in the toilets."

From a drawer, Mal pulled out a roll of tape. Grabbing one of Liberty's wrists, he taped her arm to the cage, then turned to his potions.

Liberty looked around the room. It was much messier than before. A pile of wood was in one corner, along with the pens Mal had used to make the signs. Jars were scattered instead of neatly lined up. Liberty searched for the comprehension cream among them and fixed her eyes on it. The lid was on cockeyed, as if Mal had been rushing.

"You'll be eating the pudding now, too," he said. "Just like your mother."

"What does that do?"

"It gives you a voracious appetite so all you care about is eating. I didn't want to have to feed you the way I do her, but I'll do it, and you can become a satisfied blimp too."

"It won't work. Because I won't let it."

Mal opened a jar. "Obedience ointment. This is what I rub on Sal every night while she's asleep. I hope it works better on you than it does on her."

Liberty felt her mouth drop open. So this explained

why her mother had changed so much from the one in her memories.

"Oh, don't look so shocked!" Mal opened a bottle. "It's something the pharmaceutical companies do every day, dabble with people's brains." He added a few drops into the ointment, then mixed it with a wooden stick.

"Why don't you do something useful with your friggin' genius!" Liberty yelled.

"I do. On a small island off the coast of Tasmania, there's a medicine man whose village thinks he's a god because of my telepathy tapenade. In Tibet, a whole monastery of monks can meditate for hours straight because of my brainwash bronzer. By the time they're done, they'll do whatever the Chinese government tells them. In Afghanistan, soldiers can fight for sixteen hours without having to go to the bathroom. I sell my potions on the black market for a pretty penny, and I can tell you, the money is very useful."

"I mean, use them for *good*."

"Good. Pah." Mal spat on the floor. "What do you think the authorities of this country would do if they found out about my work? Regulate it. Slap fines on me. Put the FDA, the FBI, the CIA, and the animal-rights nuts on my tail."

Liberty noticed something. Her hand was taped, but the cage could be moved. In tiny movements, she dragged it closer to the lab table. "What do you do with the money?"

"Give it to the poor, naturally." His voice dripped sarcasm.

"You're kidding?"

"Of course I'm kidding, you fool. I've *been* the poor my whole life. *What do I do?* I live it up when I'm not in this dump. Why do you think I never eat here? I wine and dine at the finest restaurants. Growing up, I had holes in my shoes. Kids made fun of me. I'm bent over because I always had to wear clothes too small for me." Mal put on a rubber glove and dipped his hand into the obedience ointment.

What if I can get it on him? Liberty thought.

Mal pulled some of the tape off her arm and pushed up her sleeve. "Now you'll be my obedient little girl."

With her free hand, Liberty slapped his face so hard, the glove flew off his hand and the jar smashed to the floor. "You'll be sorry for that. Now you're in for much worse." Mal dashed to another jar and opened it. "This will sting a little, and then it will sting a lot!"

There was a pounding upstairs.

"Someone's at the door!" Sal shouted.

"Police!" Two voices came.

"Ignore it! They'll go away," Mal yelled, but he rushed to put the lids on his jars and turn them face in.

"Open the door!" the police shouted.

A moment later, there was a cracking sound, then a smash as the front door flew off its hinges.

Welcome visitors

Mal leapt up the stairs.

Dragging the cage with her, Liberty reached the jar of comprehension cream, worked the cap off, and smoothed it on her face and hands.

Immediately, she heard a soft buzzing and humming sound coming from the far wall of the basement.

It was a legion of worms, moving through their tunnel, but she didn't have time to pay attention.

"There he is!" She heard the cabby's voice.

"My name is Officer Ham," another voice said. "And this is Officer Nickels. This gentleman says that a child was brought here against her will."

"Kidnapped!" the cabby shouted.

Mal's voice came out sweet, as Lola's had. "You must be mistaken, Officer. I merely brought my daughter home from school. She's still in her uniform."

"Why is this woman on the floor?" a second voice asked.

"She's fat, that's why," Mal said. "Once she falls, she can't get up."

"He did it!" Sal shrieked. "He made the skunk spray me."

"It doesn't smell like skunk," Officer Nickels said.

"Help the lady up," Officer Ham told him. "Would you mind producing your daughter, sir?"

"Of course. You gentlemen will wait right here. She is my lab assistant, and the lab has radioactive materials. You must wear a special suit to enter."

Liberty pushed herself away from the counter and tried to pull the cage back to where it had been.

Mal slammed down the stairs. He snatched scissors from a drawer and cut the tape off of Liberty's arm. "For your own good, and your *mother's*, keep your mouth shut!" Mal tugged her up the stairs.

The two officers stood in the living room with the cabby.

"This is my dear daughter, Libby," Mal said. "Just home from school. You know children, so belligerent. She didn't want to do her homework, so the school sent her back."

"Is this your father, little girl?" Officer Ham asked.

No, she wanted to say, but she couldn't lie to the policemen. "Yes . . . but he's a terrible father!"

Mal glared at her.

"Does he hit you?" Officer Nickels asked.

"No, but he—"

The skunk rushed up to Liberty. The officers stepped back.

"Don't spray me," Liberty shouted in her mind. "I'll help you. What did he do to you?"

The skunk hesitated. "He took me away from my family and promised if I work for him, he'll bring me back."

"He's a liar. Don't listen to him."

"Stop talking to that skunk!" Mal snapped.

The officers looked at him. "Excuse me?" Officer Ham said.

"It's *my* pet." Mal giggled. "Anyway, I have my daughter's birth certificate. Just wait here." He rushed into the kitchen.

"Don't spray us anymore and I'll help you," Liberty promised.

Mabel added her two cents. "It's what I've been telling you all along. The old man is wicked."

"It's like a regular barnyard in here," Officer Nickels said.

Liberty looked at the two officers in their uniforms. *Should I tell them about Mal's lab?* If she did, they would probably take everything away. Then she wouldn't have the comprehension cream. But she had to do something. "Downstairs," she began, "in the basement—"

"Gentlemen!" Mal dashed back in, waving two documents. He handed them to Officer Nickels. "Here is her birth certificate and my passport. As you can see, she is indeed my daughter."

"Is this *your* daughter, too?" Officer Ham asked Sal.

"Of course she's my daughter. But I wish she wasn't *his*."

"The birth certificate and passport match up," Officer Nickels said.

"A domestic dispute," Officer Ham mumbled to his partner.

"We'll just let you go back to your business." Officer Nickels gave the cabby a dirty look.

The cabby, who was very well read, quoted (in an abbreviated version) from his favorite Shakespeare play: "Something is rotten in Denmark."

Liberty's heart sank. "But he's horrible. He's going to give me a potion to make me eat."

"All parents want their children to eat," Mal said in his sweet voice.

"I just need to write down the passport number for the report," Officer Ham said. Officer Nickels handed him Mal's passport. Officer Ham pulled out a pair of reading glasses and peered at the passport, then back at Mal. "You're Mal Aimes, then?"

"Of course I'm Mal Aimes. It says so right there on my passport. Can't you read? And this is Libby Aimes, my daughter. My family and I would like to get back to our business. I shall certainly file a complaint about my door being bashed in, and I will call the cab company and have you fired, Sahib."

"*Mal* means 'evil' in French," the cabby said.

"Mal Aimes . . ." Officer Ham pulled a paper from his pocket. "I have a warrant for your arrest."

"You what?"

"Handcuffs."

"Flowers!" Mal shouted.

"Don't listen to him!" Liberty said. "He can't punish you."

"You!" Mal shouted at Liberty. "You're interrupting my communication."

Officer Nickels snapped the handcuffs on Mal's wrists.

"But I'm her father, you idiot. I told you."

"The warrant is not for kidnapping," Officer Ham explained. "The warrant is for fraud, money laundering, and tax evasion."

"Nothing about being a lousy husband?" Sal said.

"If we could arrest men for that, the jails would be overflowing."

"Who made the warrant?" Liberty had to know.

"The warrant was issued by Judge Hardnose of the district court just this morning. I'm sorry you have to see your father arrested, little girl."

I'm not! Liberty wanted to say. Instead, she winked at the cabby, who was grinning from ear to ear.

"You have the right to remain silent—"

"Someone ratted me out," Mal said. "Who ratted me out? You! Libby!"

"My name is Liberty! And from now on, I'm living up to my name!"

"Sal," Mal said, and then nodded to the cabby, "have this good man drive you to the court so you can bail me out. Write a check. The checkbook is in the drawer. I've got the money to cover bail, no matter the amount. I'll tell you where—"

Officer Ham pulled off his glasses and put them on Mal. He held the warrant up in front of Mal's face. "If you just read the bottom of Judge Hardnose's warrant, there's a little message for you."

"W-what?" Mal squinted through the thick glass.

"The fine print. At the bottom."

"'No bail,'" Mal read.

"Watch your head," Liberty reminded Mal as the officers led him out the door.

Liberty shook hands with the cabdriver and thanked him. "All in the line of duty," he said, bowing so low his turban tipped all the way to her chin. He gave her his card. "If you ever need a ride."

She stood in the doorway and watched first the cabby drive off, then Mal, who bumped his head as he got into the police car.

"What will happen to him, Liberty?" Sal came up behind her.

"I don't know, Mother. But I hope it will teach him a lesson."

Second chances

Worms don't just regenerate the soil. Worms regenerate *themselves*. The *Eisenia fetida*, for example, can regrow any parts of its body that have been cut off.

Naturally, studying these marvelous creatures had made Edgar an optimist (like Modesto Impregno). He realized that there are always second chances.

Watching Mal Aimes be dragged away by the police gave him exactly this feeling: optimism.

He didn't fret that the tunnel upon which he'd spent weeks was now useless. With Mal Aimes arrested, he could simply walk across the street like a human being, which, no offense to worms, he much preferred to be. The door was even open. He was about to dash over, but then he looked down at his clothes. He was covered in dirt, encased in mud. He could pass for a worm himself, as he once had while attending a Halloween party in Athens.

Edgar dashed to the shower and jumped in, clothes and all.

Liberty also felt cheered as she stood in her doorway looking out at the world. Judge Hardnose had paid attention to her letter. There was justice. No one would be cheated out of their insurance money after suffering a disaster, and she and her mother were free, at least until the trial.

"Is it safe out there?" Sal peered over her shoulder. "It does smell nice with all the flowers."

"Perfectly safe." Liberty took her mother's arm and led her to the old picnic table that had been cracked in two by lightning. "Mother?"

"What?"

"Did you ever used to sing me a song about stars?"

"Why, yes. It went, 'Baby wishing for a star, wishing near and far . . .'" Sal's voice was sweet, the voice in Liberty's dreams. "'Sail, my baby said, out into the sea. Only don't forget to sail back again to me.'"

"That was it." Liberty smiled.

Sal looked at the trees and bushes from her childhood. She blinked in the sun. Her stomach growled. "I'm so hungry, Liberty. I haven't eaten in days. Could you please make me some fried clams?"

"You just rest here," Liberty said. "I'll make them."

Across the street, Worm Man walked shyly through his garden toward the street. It was so lovely to see the girl close up rather than in the sky or through a window.

But who was the big blob of flesh next to her, he wondered. Where was Sally Mason?

He crossed the street and opened the creaky old gate. "Uh, hello," he called. "I am your neighbor—"

"Worm Man!" Sal shrieked, and jumped to her feet (which wasn't easy for her). "Edgar? Have you forgotten me?"

Worm Man's eyes grew wide. Could the blob be Sally Mason, the love of his life?

His first thought was to rush back into his house and lock the door, then dig a tunnel to Canada or Mexico.

His second thought was more scientific (and optimistic). He had spent years digging through the volcanic debris of Vesuvius for the fossils of ancient worms, not to mention the time spent digging his underground tunnel.

If somewhere in that mountain of sour-faced flesh was Sally Mason, he would excavate *her*!

"Hello," Liberty said. "I was just going to fry some clams for my mother. Would you like some?"

"Fried clams? Certainly not. We will have

fresh-steamed artichokes with lemon, salad from my garden drizzled with virgin olive oil from my tree, and cantaloupe, plus eight glasses of water a day. But first, some exercise. We'll start by walking around the block a few times. After that, a little yoga is in order. There will be no more fried foods or sedentary lifestyle. Do you understand, Sally Mason?"

Sal stood up, her eyes beaming. "You mean . . . you're giving me a makeover!"

"That is exactly what I mean!"

"Edgar." Sal's eyes got watery. She took Worm Man's arm.

"Are you coming on our walk?" Edgar asked Liberty, whose mouth had dropped open.

"Uh, no, thank you. I'll see to things here."

Liberty watched her mother teeter down the street on the arm of Worm Man. Sal's head was held high like a queen's.

A queen for once.

Splat! Birdbrain gave his usual announcement of arrival, right on the picnic table. "You give lousy directions," he said. "As in . . . *none*! This town has Gooch Boulevard, Gooch Avenue, and Gooch Street."

Liberty smiled. "You were so easy-going when I couldn't understand you." She put out her arm.

Birdbrain hopped on. "See my painting? I call it *Bird Contemplating His Future*."

"Very nice." Liberty frowned at the picnic table. "But don't you think the sidewalk would make a better canvas?"

"I'm too beat to make any more art. Is this home? I'll just hang here."

"You know, I think I'm beat too." Carefully avoiding Birdbrain's painting, Liberty plunked down onto the bench, wondering how the day could be more perfect.

Of course, she didn't know that Ms. Klaus, application in hand, was driving swiftly through the city on her way. Her navigation, though, was much worse than Birdbrain's; she'd already gotten lost twice.

Birdbrain hopped down and wandered around the yard. He had his own interest in worms, unscientific.

Bricks

The drawers in the mind are interesting.

Some are easy to open. Like the drawer with your best friend's name in it. Some are harder to nudge, like the answer to a question on a test.

Then there are drawers that open on their own time. These drawers have jewels in them: the diamonds of imagination, the rubies of memory, the sapphires of dreams, the tiny pearls of wisdom. Getting them open is tricky.

But there is one thing you can do to unlock them: absolutely nothing. Stare into space. Glance out the window. Gaze at the horizon. Watch the stars.

That is what happened to Liberty. Sitting on the broken bench in her yard, enjoying the trees and flowers and sky, she felt a drawer open in her mind.

It was something the snake had told her: *The evil one hides green papers behind the bricks.*

So much had happened that day when she let out the animals and flew away, that she had forgotten.

Green papers? Does that mean money?

It had always been a mystery that Mal could work so many hours, yet never have enough money to buy anything: not a toy, or a book, or a new carpet. Just the food Sal ate.

"Write a check to bail me out," he'd told Sal. That meant there was money in the bank, but was he also hiding money in the walls? Money for the Sullivan School?

"I'm going inside," she told Birdbrain. "Do you want to come?"

"I'll hang here in the sunshine."

Without Mal, the house was already more cheerful. Light poured in through the open door. Mabel and Flowers dozed on the couch.

There was so much to do: send Birdbrain for No Name, and have him bring a note to Ms. Klaus. Maybe the neighbor even had a phone.

But first . . . green papers.

Every single wall of the basement was brick. But Liberty was experienced with bricks. As she felt along, tugging and prying, she came to a realization: *My life is as interesting as a book!*

She couldn't wait to turn the page, to find out: *What happens next?*

Acknowledgments

A book is a collaborative process. For their encouragement and help in revising this book, I would like to thank Isaac Robert Easton Spivack; Michael Ruben; Randi Easton Wickham; my agent, Michael Bourret; and my editors, Wendy Lamb and Caroline Meckler.

216-

Kelly Easton is the author of *White Magic*, the Betts Pets series, and several novels for young adults, including *The Life History of a Star*, *Walking on Air*, *Aftershock*, *Hiroshima Dreams*, and *To Be Mona*. Her books have received several honors, among them an Asian/Pacific American Award for Literature, a Golden Kite Honor, a Julia Ward Howe Honor, the ASTAL Rhode Island Middle School Book of the Year award, and a Chapel Hill Public Library Best Book award, and have been Book Sense, New York Public Library Books for the Teen Age, and Kentucky Bluegrass Master List selections. Kelly is on the faculty of the MFA in Writing for Children and Young Adults Program at Hamline University. She lives in Rhode Island and Massachusetts with her husband, Michael Ruben, and their children. You can visit her on the Web at kellyeaston.com.